Who wanted to censor William Shakespeare, Benjamin Franklin, Walt Whitman, and a host of other great writers? And what was it that they wanted to censor?

The answers are in *Banned: Classical Erotica*, a collection of ribald and erotic excerpts that ran afoul of the bluenoses. It's a fascinating chronicle of the centuries-old campaign to rein in great minds—and a reminder that, in the long run, great minds tend to win.

BANNED: Classical Erotica

BANNED: Classical Erotica

Forty sensual and erotic excerpts from Aristophanes to Whitman—uncensored.

Victor Gulotta & Brandon Toropov

BOB ADAMS, INC.
PUBLISHERS
Holbrook, Massachusetts

Published by Bob Adams, Inc.
260 Center Street, Holbrook, MA 02343

ISBN: 1-55850-109-6

Printed in the United States of America

B   C   D   E   F   G   H   I   J

For Orrin and Jesse

✳   ✳   ✳

"The dirtiest book in all the world is
an expurgated book."
                                    — *Walt Whitman*

Table of Contents

✳   ✳   ✳

Acknowledgments

Although it was rewarding and great fun, assembling this book was a difficult and occasionally odd experience we couldn't have managed alone. For his help in combing the shelves of the Boston, Brookline, and Cambridge Public Libraries, Peter Weiss deserves a thousand thanks and a lifetime reprieve from the suspicious eyebrow-raisings of those who control access to the "forbidden stacks." Lynne Griffin took time out to help us narrow down the candidates—we owe thanks to her and to Gigi Ranno for not minding that we were destroying their schedule. Donna Gulotta and Mary Toropov each contributed valuable insights and no small amount of patience during this project. James D'Entremont of the Boston Coalition for Freedom of Expression provided a great deal of important information, and, more important, positive vibrations aplenty—though it's out of style to say so. Dan Caldwell gave us the story about Harry Stephens and a lifetime's worth of lessons about the theatre. Bernie Rath at the American Booksellers Association offered advice and direction, and we thank him. Dawn Hobson was her usual tireless, detail-oriented self, for which many thanks are in order. Christopher Ciaschini put up with enormous changes at the last minute for the (fill in the blank) time, and we are deeply grateful. Bob Adams provided flexibility and moral support. Wayne Jackson served as house curmudgeon and we wouldn't want it any other way.

Introduction

"It breeds lust. Lust defiles the body, debauches the imagination, corrupts the mind, deadens the will, destroys the memory, sears the conscience, hardens the heart, and damns the soul . . . . This traffic has made rakes and libertines in our society—skeletons in many a household. The family is polluted, homes desecrated and each generation born into the world is more and more cursed by the inherited weakness, the harvest of this seed-sowing of the Evil One."

— *Anthony Comstock* 19th-century moral crusader, on "morally offensive literature."

✳   ✳   ✳

Anthony Comstock felt so strongly about the pernicious nature of certain works of literature that he sought legislation to ban their translation into English. Such an idea is laughable today—or is it?

We assembled this collection because we felt that Comstock's present-day successors—and there are plenty—have only grown more subtle. Their basic motivations remain the same: to apply the values and preconceptions of a minority in such a way that the majority is denied free access to thoughts and ideas. This book is meant to show that their old tricks are just that—old— and that, regardless of the guise in which it is presented, officially sanctioned suppression of ideas is a plan doomed to fail in a progressive secular society such as ours. Our book features, in chronological order, brief and unapologetic excerpts of notable ribaldry from dozens of classic authors whose works faced suppression or censorship.

✳   ✳   ✳

Censors invariably view their work as something other than what it is. Most of the passages in this book were, at one time, altered or suppressed in the name of either "improving" the text in question or "protecting" the morals of the reader who would never get to see it. It is fashionable today to reject such paternalistic nonsense when assessing the (mercifully concluded) excesses of Communist regimes. Yet it is quite common to hear arguments that run along similar lines in debates about the National Endowment for the Arts. If we cannot learn from our own mistakes, we might cast an objective eye to the errors of the enemy we have overcome.

To our way of thinking, trying to keep people from reading, writing, or thinking about subjects like sex and sensuality is a fool's gambit. Such maneuvers are cloaked in high-minded terms appealing to decorum and responsibility but this is typically an effort to mask their inherent absurdity.

Not too many years ago, words like "bed," "cuckold," and "hot" were systematically excised from the works of Shakespeare by the estimable Dr. Thomas Bowdler and his legions of imitators. All of them thought themselves to be doing the Bard a great service by pruning his perceived "defects." Some of these editions were known, in the unintentionally deft phrasing of the day, as "gelded" or "castrated" editions; others took the self-defeating step of placing spicy passages in italics so as to alert the reader to skip over them when reading aloud. Each approach—rewriting and highlighting—only serves to subvert the objective of the text and call attention to what has been tampered with. The "corrected" editions simply don't represent what Shakespeare wrote, and that is reason enough to reject them.

Bowdler's day eventually passed—Jesse Helms's will, as well. We must remember that censorship is perhaps as old as literature itself—Ovid ran afoul of the Emperor Augustus before he horrified editors and librarians. In a world in which Anne Frank's *Diary of a Young Girl* is kept off the shelves of high school libraries on the grounds of "decency," it's worth remembering that prudes, opportunists, and self-serving politicians have always been with us. Many, many masterworks faced attacks from the self-appointed morals guardians of the day. All too often, they still do.

Art has a way of winning, over time, its battles with censors. *Banned: Classical Erotica* charts some of the notable conflicts, and sets out to demonstrate what most of us know already: that sensual and erotic writing is a legitimate form of literary expression that is as valid, entertaining, and profound as any other area of human discourse—and as old as the Bible and the comedies of ancient Greece.

Like many other Americans, we are uneasy about today's ever more daring inroads against freedom of expression. We offer this book, which contains excerpts from the works of William Shakespeare, Walt Whitman, Geoffrey Chaucer, Aristophanes, and a host of other writers likely to shake the foundations of the republic and undermine public morals, as an object lesson to today's Anthony Comstocks and Thomas Bowdlers.

It is regrettable that, in this age, it should still be necessary to argue against literary and artistic censorship. But generations of censors have left a black legacy that won't disappear, making this book a necessity. Lastly, we note with both defiance and a certain satisfaction that assembling this book was a lot of fun. We trust that reading it will be, too.

— *B.T. & V.G*

Note

The authors have provided their own working translations and adaptations for the selections that feature *The Greek Anthology*, *Lysistrata*, *The Art of Love*, *The Decameron*, *The Origin of Manabozho*, and *Partie Carrée*.

FROM

The Greek Anthology

This varied collection of short epigrams and public inscriptions, some of which date as early as 700 B.C., was assembled over a period of centuries by succeeding generations of Greek editors and writers.

Around 1000 A.D., a scholar by the name of Cephalas made the first notable attempt to formally organize the centuries-old verses. Four hundred years later, a monk called Planudes prepared a revision of Cephalas's work that was acceptable to his superiors in the Church. Virtually all of the verses that dealt with eroticism were excised—and suppressed for the next four centuries.

＊　＊　＊

TO A POMPOUS CENSOR
> You sneerer at the sight of love, who looks to bust
> With haughtiness, recall, as those who die proud
> > must,
> Your very life you owe—thank all the gods—to lust.
> —*Palladas*

* * *

SUCH A PITY

Why does a man seek whores? The answer's easy.
He'd much prefer the true-love to the sleazy,
And would long for his betrothed as when a suitor
If a woman's charms remained after he'd screwed
    her.
    —Rufinus

* * *

THE UNLUCKY PAINTER

That Eutychus did portraits in the town:
Had twenty sons, set not one likeness down.
    —Lucilius

ARISTOPHANES

Lysistrata

Aristophanes' *Lysistrata* is among the most popular plays in the history of the theater; many scholars consider it the greatest of the ancient Greek comedies. The following scene was, some years back, the cause of an obscenity proceeding against the Los Angeles backers of a low-budget production of the play. As one actor tells the story, a policeman stopped the performance, dismissed the audience, and loaded the cast members into a paddy wagon. Upon reaching the station house, he dutifully booked the actors and took fingerprints, then asked where he could locate the playwright, Harry Stephens. The actors had to inform him that Mr. Stephens, or Aristophanes as he was known to his friends, had been dead for nearly three thousand years.

The plot of the play involves a sex strike by both Athenian and Spartan women, who are intent on securing a peace treaty by depriving their warring husbands of love. Such direct treatment of sensual matters is common for Aristophanes and, even today, a controversial point for publishers and scholars. Virtually all published editions of Aristophanes' play *The Knights* are expurgated to one degree or another.

✳ ✳ ✳

LYSISTRATA: Girls! Come here quickly!

A WOMAN: What?

LYSISTRATA: Here comes a man—bulging at his seams with love. Oh, Aphrodite, Paphian, Kythereian, heed us and grant us your aid.

A WOMAN: The enemy? Where?

LYSISTRATA: There, by the shrine of Demeter.

A WOMAN: Good God, you're right. Who on earth . . . ?

MYRRHINE: It's my husband Kinesias!

LYSISTRATA: Well, then: get to work. Tempt him! Torture him! Destroy him! Give him what he wants—kisses, tickles, caresses, all the rest of your arsenal—but stop short, and do not give him the last prize, that which we swore on the wine to withhold.

MYRRHINE: Count on it.

LYSISTRATA: I will. Now then; I'll prime the pump for you. The rest of you withdraw.

(KINESIAS enters with a huge erection.)

KINESIAS: God . . . Oh, God . . . I'm hard-up for lack of exercise. I'll stand for awhile, it's all I can manage.

LYSISTRATA: Halt! Who goes there?

KINESIAS: It's me.

LYSISTRATA: A man?

KINESIAS (Motioning toward his bulge): You have to ask?

LYSISTRATA: Get out.

KINESIAS: Says who?

LYSISTRATA: Says the Officer of the Day.

KINESIAS: Officer, I'm begging you—let Myrrhine come to me. By all the gods above, I implore you.

LYSISTRATA: Myrrhine, eh? Mind if I ask your name, sir?

KINESIAS: I'm Kinesias. Her husband.

LYSISTRATA: Oh, pardon me! You're welcome here, of course. We've heard about you. That Myrrhine, she's always on about you. She can't so much as nibble any of the foods of love without sighing, "Here's to my own Kinesias!"

KINESIAS: Oh, dear God. Get her down here immediately, then.

LYSISTRATA: What's in it for me?

KINESIAS: We may settle that later—by coming to a standing agreement.

LYSISTRATA: I'll see what I can do. (She exits.)

KINESIAS: Hurry! Oh, gods above, what is life worth without a woman? I can't eat a thing. I can't sleep. I walk in the house and it's so depressing I can hardly . . . hardly *stand* it. Love is going to be the death of me. Hurry! Hurry!

(MANES, a slave, enters, carrying KINESIAS'S infant.)

MYRRHINE (offstage): You know how much I love him! I worship him! the problem is, he hates the idea of touching me! No, I won't do it. I'm staying here. (She enters above him, at a balcony.)

KINESIAS (Catching sight of her): Myrrhine! My little Myrrhine! My darling! Come down here, and hurry!

MYRRHINE: I'm afraid that's impossible.

KINESIAS: What? Why, Myrrhine?

MYRRHINE: Why? Because you don't need me.

KINESIAS: Don't need you? For God's sake, *look* at me!

MYRRHINE: Goodbye now. (She makes to leave.)

KINESIAS: Myrrhine! Wait! If you won't come down

for me, at least think of the child! (He pinches the baby.) Hey, you: let's hear it now.

THE BABY: Mommy! Mommy!

KINESIAS: There! You hear? It's pathetic. Six whole days without a bath, can you believe that? Not a bite for the little tyke. It's heartbreaking, isn't it?

MYRRHINE: Oh, my baby! What a father you have!

KINESIAS: Come down. For the baby.

MYRRHINE: I imagine I have no choice. What a life, being a mother!

(She enters.)

KINESIAS: How lovely she looks! And she seems so much younger now! The worse she treats me, the more hot and bothered I get.

MYRRHINE: My sweet baby. You're as delightful as your daddy is wicked. Kiss, kiss.

KINESIAS: Surely you must see now what a mistake it was to get mixed up in this League of Women business. It's no good for either of us.

MYRRHINE: Hands off!

KINESIAS: But our home! It's disintegrating!

MYRRHINE: Who cares?

KINESIAS: The chickens! They've been tearing your knitting to pieces! Surely you must feel some—

MYRRHINE: No. None.

KINESIAS: Well—what about that which we owe to Aphrodite? Please, please come back.

MYRRHINE: No. Not unless all of you men sit down, conclude a treaty, and put an end to this war.

KINESIAS: That's certainly possible. Yes. We could manage that.

MYRRHINE: Really? Well, I could be persuaded in that case. Until then, however, I'm under oath not to yield to you.

KINESIAS: Oh, don't bother about that. Now, then—

MYRRHINE: No! Hey! I said hands off!—But you know I love you, don't you?

KINESIAS: Yes, yes. Now, my dear: Let's proceed.

MYRRHINE: In front of the baby? You're mad!

KINESIAS: Manes, take the baby home. (MANES leaves with the baby.)

MYRRHINE: You're wicked. Where did you intend to go?

KINESIAS: Some nice tight spot. Pan's cave, perhaps.

MYRRHINE: Aren't you forgetting about my purification before I return to the citadel?

KINESIAS: We'll dunk you in the sacred springs while no one's looking.

MYRRHINE: What about my oath?

KINESIAS: Don't bother your head about that. I'm still the man in this household.

MYRRHINE: Oh . . . all right. If you say so. Let me go find us a bed.

KINESIAS: To hell with the bed. This ground's just fine. Come on.

MYRRHINE: Oh, I wouldn't dream of it. You're a devil, but you deserve better than the cold earth. (She exits.)

KINESIAS: My love. How considerate she is to me!

MYRRHINE: (Re-entering.) Your bed, sir. Now, let me just slip these clothes off, and . . . Wait! There's no mattress!

KINESIAS: We don't need it. Forget about it.

MYRRHINE: I couldn't! To do it just sprawled out on blankets? It's tawdry.

KINESIAS: Kiss me now. Please.

MYRRHINE: I won't be a moment. (She exits.)

KINESIAS: I swear I am going to explode right here.

MYRRHINE: (Re-entering.) Your mattress. Now, all that's left is for me to get this dress off, and we can . . . oh, look! No pillow.

KINESIAS: I don't need a pillow.

MYRRHINE: What about me? (She exits.)

KINESIAS: Heracles himself would be unable to take this.

MYRRHINE (Re-entering.) All set. Here we go.

KINESIAS: All set, yes. Come, lie down.

MYRRHINE: Just let me get this underwear off. Oh, but hold on: you'll remember your promise to me about the treaty?

KINESIAS: Oh, yes. Definitely.

MYRRHINE: The bedspread! Where is it?

KINESIAS: I'll be your bedspread. Come here.

MYRRHINE: Hold on a second. (She exits.)

KINESIAS: The woman and her damned bedspreads. I can't take it!

MYRRHINE: (Re-entering) Here we are. Just get up for a minute.

KINESIAS: I've been *up* for some time already.

MYRRHINE: Want some scent before we do it?

KINESIAS: In Apollo's name, no!

MYRRHINE: In Aphrodite's name, yes! I don't care what you say about it. (She exits.)

KINESIAS: Hurry, love. Hurry!

MYRRHINE: (Re-entering.) Here, give me your hand. Rub it in like this.

KINESIAS: I never liked scent. And this is so strong! Still . . .

MYRRHINE: Oh, what an idiot I am! This is the Rhodian bottle.

KINESIAS: It's fine! Honest!

MYRRHINE: No, I don't mind. Just wait right here. (She exits.)

KINESIAS: If I ever get my hands on the man who invented scent ...

MYRRHINE: (Re-entering.) Finally. The bottle I wanted.

KINESIAS: *I've* got the bottle you want, and it's right here and ready to pour. My love, please, don't bother about any more trifles. Come lie with me.

MYRRHINE: Of course. Just let me slip off my shoes. Oh, about that treaty—you will vote in favor of it?

KINESIAS: We'll see.

(MYRRHINE exits.)

She's gone! The woman gets me all hot, damn her, she nearly has me keeling over, and she runs away. What will I do? How am I going to get any now?

(To his penis:)

And you, my throbbing little friend, what will become of you? We should both be in the clinic!

OVID

The Art of Love

Ovid was banished from Rome for writing this book, and
for some other indiscretion that irked the Emperor Augustus but has been lost to history. The book of verse—
which offers not only advice, but also a fascinating look at
the Roman sexual mores of the time—has earned scores
of detractors who followed in the footsteps of Augustus.
The poet's works were publicly burned in the bonfire of
Savonarola in Rome in 1497; as recently as 1928, the
U.S. Customs Service was seizing copies of *The Art of
Love* at the border.

In the following passage, the poet offers some ro-
mantic pointers to an elite female readership.

*   *   *

We've cruised enough byways. I have to bring this
tired boat into port safely, so I must attack the naked facts
of the matter.

You eagerly await an escort to all the parties; in this,
too, you desire my counsel. Very well—show up late,

when the lamps have been lit; make your entrance a graceful one. Making them wait will add to your enticements; anticipation makes a great brothel-keeper. Perhaps your looks are plain; in the evening, you'll look great to the man who's had a few belts. Low lights and shadows will be most forgiving to your faults.

Eat like a lady; politeness and good manners count. Don't sup at home first and then eat little crumbs all night. By the same token, don't overeat; save some room. Suppose Paris saw Helen gorging herself; he'd think her boorish, he'd consider the trouble he took abducting her a major error.

Drink, however, is another story (for girls, that is). It's right for them; ardor and wine complement each other well. And don't forget that a good set of brains will guarantee you sound walking and clear thought: no blurry double vision! Ah, but the girl who falls down drunk is a loathsome sight, and she deserves to be mounted by anyone in the room. It's every bit as dangerous to fall asleep as the table's being cleared: the girl who snores thus may find herself in a penetrating situation.

What remains must be told with a blush. Yet Venus, the kind one, calls her own all that makes us blush. Each woman must come to know herself, and ought to select the ways most appropriate to her own body. There is no one way for all.

The girl whose face is lovely should lie on her back; the one whose hindquarters are her prime asset should present that view. You'll recall that Milanion took Atalanta's legs on his shoulders; this is the method for women whose legs are pleasant. Little ones should "stride the horse" (though Hector's bride in Thebes, Andromache, was too tall to play this game, and made a poor jockey).

Let's say yours is the lean and lithe figure, the figure of the clothes-model; kneel on your bed, with your neck arched up slightly. The one with perfect legs and breasts should lie down sideways and make her partner stand. Don't be bashful; let your hair down like some love-crazed maenad, let the locks fall enticingly along the curve of your throat. Has childbirth creased your belly? Do as the Parthians do, and make yours a rear action.

There are innumerable positions for making love—one simple and easy one is to lie supine on your right side, reclining halfway. You will find more truth in my Muse than from Delphi or Ammon; experience tells. Put your trust in my art, and follow these verses to the letter! A woman should feel the ecstasy deep in her bones; love-making should satisfy both partners equally.

OVID
(Translated by John Dryden)

Amours

Sir Walter Scott first began work on an edition of Dryden's works in 1805. In it he reprinted the following translation of Ovid, which had been left out of rival editor John Warton's editions. He did so not without some severe misgivings, however; one letter to a colleague notes that "there are some passages . . . that will hardly bear reprinting unless I would have the Bishop of London and the whole corps of Methodists about my ears."

Even with such premonitions of disaster, Scott took the risk and printed a truly complete edition of Dryden—the first.

❋   ❋   ❋

Book I, Elegy 4
To his mistress, whose husband is invited to a feast with
them. The poet instructs her how to behave in his company.

Your husband will be with us at the treat;
May that be the last supper he shall eat!
And am poor I, a guest invited there
Only to see, while he may touch the fair?
To see you kiss and hug your nauseous lord,
While his lewd hand descends below the board?
Now wonder not that Hippodamia's charms,
At such a sight, the centaurs urged to arms;
That in a rage they threw their cups aside,
Assailed the bridegroom, and would force the bride.
I am not half a horse, (I would I were!)
Yet hardly can from you my hands forbear.
Take then my counsel; which, observed, may be
Of some importance both to you and me.
Be sure to come before your man be there;
There's nothing can be done; but come, howe'er.
Sit next him, (that belongs to decency),
But tread upon my foot in passing by;
Read in my looks what silently they speak,
And slily, with your eyes, your answer make.
My lifted eyebrow shall declare my pain;
My right hand to his fellow shall complain,
And on the back a letter shall design,
Besides a note that shall be writ in wine.
Whene'er you think upon our last embrace,
With your forefinger gently touch your face;
If any word of mine offend my dear,
Pull with your hand the velvet of your ear;
If you are pleased with what I do or say,

Handle your rings, or with your fingers play.
As suppliants use at altars, hold the board,
Whene'er you wish the devil may take your lord.
When he fills for you, never touch the cup,
But bid the officious cuckold drink it up.
The waiter on those services employ;
Drink you, and I will snatch it from the boy,
Watching the part where your sweet mouth hath
      been,
And thence with eager lips will suck it in.
If he, with clownish manners, thinks it fit
To taste, and offer you the nasty bit,
Reject his greasy kindness, and restore
The unsavoury morsel he had chewed before.
Nor let his arms embrace your neck, nor rest
Your tender cheek upon his hairy breast;
Let not his hand within your bosom stray,
And rudely with your pretty bubbies play;
But above all let him no kiss receive!
That's an offence I never can forgive.
Do not, O do not that sweet mouth resign,
Lest I rise up in arms and cry, "'Tis mine."
I shall thrust in betwixt, and, void of fear,
The manifest adulterer will appear.
These things are plain to sight; but more I doubt
What you conceal beneath your petticoat.
Take not his leg between your tender thighs,
Nor with your hand provoke my foe to rise.
How many love inventions I deplore,
Which I myself have practiced all before!
How oft have I been forced the robe to lift
In company; to make a homely shift
For a bare bout, ill huddled o'er in haste,
While o'er my side the fair her mantle cast!

You to your husband shall not be so kind;
But, lest you should, your mantle leave behind.
Encourage him to tope; but kiss him not,
Nor mix one drop of water in his pot.
If he be fuddled well, and snores apace,
Then we may take advice from time and place.
When all depart, while compliments are loud,
Be sure to mix among the thickest crowd;
There I will be, and there we cannot miss,
Perhaps to grubble, or at least to kiss.
Alas! what length of labour I employ,
Just to secure a short and transient joy!
For night must part us; and when night is come,
Tucked underneath his arms he leads you home.
He locks you in; I follow to the door,
His fortune envy, and my own deplore.
He kisses you, he more than kisses too;
The outrageous cuckold thinks it all his due.
But add not to his joy by your consent,
And let it not be given, but only lent.
Return no kiss, nor move in any sort;
Make it a dull and a malignant sport.
Had I my wish, he should no pleasure take,
But slubber o'er your business for my sake;
And whate'er fortune shall this night befall,
Coax me tomorrow, by forswearing all.

PETRONIUS

The Satyricon

Here we have an excellent example of how a decorous, high-minded translation of a classic confronts the original author's unapologetic sensuality. There follow two translations of the same verses from Petronius's satiric portrait of debauchery in Nero's Rome, *The Satyricon*. The first, completed in 1922, was the work of W.C. Firebaugh. The second is a 1959 translation by William Arrowsmith.

The Satyricon is a frank, often unashamedly lewd piece of work that traces the wanderings of an educated rogue and his serving boy through a maze of carnal and material excesses. You be the judge of which of the two poems that follow best captures Petronius's spirit—and the mores of the times in which he lived.

✳   ✳   ✳

FIREBAUGH

Tither, hither quickly gather, pathic companions
  boon;
Artfully stretch forth your limbs and on with the
  dance and play!
Twinkling feet and supple thighs and agile buttocks
  in tune,
Hands well skilled in raising passions, Delian
  Eunuchs gay!

ARROWSMITH

O fairies, O buggers,
  O eunuchs exotic!
Come running, come running,
  ye anal-erotic!

With soft little hands,
  with flexible bums,
Come, O castrati,
  unnatural ones!

The Golden Ass

Apuleius, a respected scholar and attorney, wove the ideas of earlier Roman authors into his masterwork, *The Golden Ass*, which in turn influenced such writers as Boccaccio and LeSage. The book describes the author's supposed travels into Thessaly, where he is transformed by witches into an ass. It is, of course, a work of fantasy, but many scholars have found autobiographical elements in its lines. Apuleius was, for instance, accused of sorcery in a messy legal squabble; the case—in which he acted as his own lawyer—was resolved in his favor.

Even though this book had been readily and legally available in the United States for some years, customs officials raised an import ban on it in the early 1930s.

* * *

HOW APULEIUS FELL IN LOVE WITH FOTIS

When I was within the house I found my dear and sweet love, Fotis, mincing meat and making pottage for her master and mistress. The cupboard was all set with wines, and I thought I smelled the savor of some dainty meats. She had about her middle a white and clean apron, and she was girded about her body under her breast with a swathe of red silk, and she stirred the pot and turned the meat with her fair and white hands in such sort that it was in my mind a comely sight to see.

These things when I saw I was half amazed, and stood musing with myself, and my courage came then upon me, which before was scant. And I spoke to Fotis plainly, and said, "O Fotis, how trimly you can stir the pot, and how finely you can make pottage. Oh, happy and twice happy is he to whom you give leave and license but to touch you."

Then she, being likewise wittily disposed, answered, "Depart, I say, wretch, from me, depart from my fire, for if the flame thereof do never so little blaze forth, it will burn thee extremely: and none can extinguish the heat thereof but I alone."

When she had said these words, she cast her eyes upon me and laughed, but I did not depart from thence until such time as I had viewed her in every point. But what should I speak of others? I do accustom abroad to mark and view the face and hair of every dame, and afterward delight myself therewith privately at home, and thereby judge the residue of their shape, because the face is the principal part of all the body, and is first open to our eyes, and whatsoever flourishing and gorgeous apparel doth work and set forth in the corporal parts of a woman, the same doth the natural and comely beauty set out in the face. Moreover, there are some who (to the intent to show their grace and feature) will case off their partlets, collars, habiliments, fronts, cornets, and crepines, and delight more to show the fairness of their skin than to deck themselves up in gold and precious stones. But because it is a crime to me to say so, and to give no example thereof, know ye that if you spoil and cut off the hair of any woman or deprive her of the color of her face, though she were never so excellent in beauty, though she were thrown down from heaven, sprung of the seas, nourished of the floods, though she were Venus herself, though she were accompanied with the Graces, though she were waited upon of all the court of Cupid, though she were girded with her beautiful scarf of love, and though she smelled of perfumes and musks, yet if she appeared bald, she could in no wise please, no, not her own Vulcan.

Oh how well doth a fair color and a shining face agree with glittering hair! Behold, it encounters with the beams of the sun, and pleases the eye marvelously. Sometimes the beauty of the hair resembles the color of gold and honey, sometimes the blue plume and azure feathers about the necks of doves, especially when it is either anointed with the gum of Arabia or trimly tufted out with the teeth of a fine comb; if it be tied up in the nape of the neck, it seems to the lover who beholds it as a glass yielding forth a more pleasant and gracious comeliness than if it were sparsed abroad on the shoulders of the woman or hung down scattering behind. Finally, there is such a dignity in the hair, that whatsoever she be, though she be never so bravely attired with gold, silks, precious stones, and other rich and gorgeous ornaments, yet if her hair be not curiously set forth, she cannot seem fair.

But in my Fotis her garments unbraced and unlaced did increase her beauty. Her hair hung about her shoulders, and was dispersed abroad upon her partlet, and on every part of her neck, howbeit the greater part was trussed up in her nape with a lace. Then I, unable to withstand the broiling heat I was in, ran upon her and kissed the place where she had thus laid her hair; whereat she turned her face, and cast her rolling eyes upon me, saying, "O scholar, thou hast tasted now both honey and gall; take heed that thy pleasure do not turn into repentance."

"Tush" (quoth I), "my sweetheart, I am contented, for such another kiss, to be broiled here upon this fire." Wherewithal I embraced and kissed her more often, and she embraced and kissed me likewise. Her breath smelled like cinnamon, and the liquor of her tongue was like sweet nectar. Wherewith when my mind was greatly delighted, I said, "Behold, Fotis, I am yours, and shall presently die, unless you take pity upon me." Which when I had said, she eftsoons kissed me and bid me be of good courage, and, "I will" (quoth she) "satisfy your whole desire, and it shall be no longer delayed than until night. Wherefore go your ways and prepare yourself."

Thus when we have lovingly talked and reasoned together, we departed for that time . . .

When noon was come, Byrrhena sent me a fat pig, five hens, and a flagon of old wine. Then I called Fotis and said, "Behold how Bacchus the egger and stirrer of love offers himself of his own accord. Let us therefore drink up this wine, that we may prepare ourselves."

It fortuned on a day that Byrrhena desired me earnestly to sup with her, and she would in no wise take any excuse. Whereupon I went to Fotis to ask counsel of her, as of some divine, who (although she was unwilling that I should depart one foot from her company) yet at length she gave me license to be absent for a while, saying, "Beware that you tarry not long at supper there, for there is a rabblement of common rioters and disturbers of the public peace that rove about in the streets, and murder all such as they may take; neither can law nor justice redress them in any case. And they will the sooner set upon you, by reason of your comeliness and audacity, in that you are not afraid at any time to walk in the streets."

Then I answered and said, "Have no care of me, Fotis, for I esteem the pleasure which I have with thee above the dainty meats that I eat abroad, and therefore I will return again quickly. Nevertheless I mind not to come without company, for I have here my sword, whereby I hope to defend myself."

After dining I arose from the table and took leave of Byrrhena. When I came into the first street my torch went out, and I could scarce get home by reason it was so dark and I had to move slowly, for fear of stumbling.

When I was well-nigh come to the door I saw three men of great stature heaving and lifting at Milo's gates to get in. And when they saw me they were nothing afraid, but essayed with more force to break down the doors, whereby they gave me occasion (and not without cause) to think that they were strong thieves. Whereupon I drew out my sword, which I carried under my cloak, and ran in among them, and wounded them in such sort that they fell down dead before my face. Thus when I had slain them all, I knocked, sweating and breathing at the door, till Fotis let me in. And then, full weary with the slaughter of these thieves, like Hercules when he fought against King Gerion, I went to my chamber and laid me down to sleep.

When I was abed I began to call to mind all the sorrows and griefs that I was in the day before, until such time as my love Fotis came into the chamber, not as she was wont to do, for she seemed nothing pleasant either in countenance or talk, but with a sour face and frowning look. She began to speak in this sort: "Verily, I confess that I have been the occasion of all thy trouble this day."

Therewithal she pulled out a whip from under her apron, and delivered it to me, saying, "Revenge thyself of me, or rather slay me. And think you not that I willingly procured this anguish and sorrow to you, I call the gods to witness. I had rather suffer my own body to be punished than that you should receive or sustain any harm by my means. That which I did was by the commandment of another, and wrought (as I thought) for some other, but behold, the unlucky chance fortuned on you by my evil occasion."

I, very curious and desirous to know the matter, answered, "In faith" (quoth I), "this most pestilent and evil-favored whip (which thou hast brought to scourge thee withal) shall first be broken in a thousand pieces than that it should touch or hurt thy delicate and dainty skin. But I pray you tell me, how have you been the cause and means of my trouble and sorrow? For I dare swear by the love that I bear to you (and I will not be persuaded, though you yourself should endeavor the same) that ever you went about to trouble or harm me. Perhaps sometimes you imagined an evil thought in your mind, which afterward you revoked; but that is not to be deemed as a crime."

When I had spoken these words, I perceived by Fotis's eyes being wet with tears, and well-nigh closed up, that she had a desire to pleasure, and specially because she embraced and kissed me sweetly. And when she was somewhat restored to joy, she desired me that she might first shut the chamber door, lest by the intemperance of her tongue in uttering any unfitting words there might grow further inconvenience. Wherewithal she barred and propped the door and came to me again, and embracing me lovingly about the neck with both her arms, spoke with a soft voice, and said, "I do greatly fear to discover the privities of this house, and to utter the secret mysteries of my dame. But I have a confidence in you and your wisdom, by reason that you are come of so noble a line and endued with so profound sapience, and are further instructed in so many holy and divine things, so that you will faithfully keep silence, and whatsoever I shall reveal or declare unto you, you would close within the bottom of your heart, and never discover the same: for I assure the love that I bear to you enforces me to utter it. Now shall you know all the estate of our house; now shall you know the hidden secrets of my mistress, whom the powers of hell do obey, and by whom the celestial planets are troubled, the gods made weak, and the elements subdued; neither is the violence of her art in more strength and force than when she espies some comely young man who pleases her fancy, as oftentimes it happens. For now she loves one Boeotian, a fair and beautiful person, on whom she employs all her sorcery and enchantment; and I heard her say with my own ears yesternight that (if the sun had not then gone down, and the night come to minister convenient time to work her magical enticements) she would have brought perpetual darkness over all the world herself. You shall know that when she saw yesternight this Boeotian sitting at the barber's, when she came from the baths, she secretly commanded me to gather some of the hair of his head, which lay dispersed upon the ground, and to bring it home; which when I thought to have done, the barber espied me, and by reason it was bruited throughout all the city that we were witches and enchantresses, he cried out, and said, 'Will you never leave off stealing of young men's hairs? In faith, I assure you unless you cease your wicked sorceries I will complain to the justices.'

"With that he came angrily toward me, and took away the hair which I had gathered out of my apron, which grieved me very much, for I knew my mistress's manners, that she would not be contented, but beat me cruelly. Wherefore I intended to run away, but the remembrance of you put always that thought out of my mind, and so I came homeward very sorrowfully; but because I would not seem to come in my mistress's sight with empty hands, I saw a man shearing blown goat skins, and the hair that he had shorn off was yellow, and much resembled the hair of the Boeotian.

"I took a good deal thereof and, coloring the matter, brought it to my mistress. When night came, before your return from supper, she (to bring her purpose to pass) went up to a high gallery of her house, opening to the east part of the world, and, preparing herself according to her accustomed practice, she gathered together all her substance for fumigations. She brought forth plates of metal carved with strange characters, she prepared the bones of such as were drowned by tempest in the seas, she made ready the members of dead men, as their nostrils and fingers. She set out the lumps of flesh of such as were hanged, the blood which she had reserved of such as were slain, and the jawbones and teeth of wild beasts. Then she said certain charms over the hair, and dipped it in divers waters, as in well water, cow's milk, mountain honey, and other liquor, which, when she had done, she tied and lapped up together, and with many perfumes and smells threw it into a hot fire to burn.

"Then by the great force of this sorcery, and the violence of so many confections, those bodies (whose hair was burning in the fire) received human shape, and felt, heard, and walked, and (smelling the scent of their own hair) came and rapped at our doors instead of Boeotius. Then you, being well tippled, and deceived by the obscurity of the night, drew out your sword courageously, like furious Ajax, and killed, not as he did, the whole herd of beasts, but three blown skins."

When I was thus pleasantly mocked and taunted by Fotis, I said to her, "Verily, now may I for this achieved enterprise be numbered as Hercules, who by his valiant prowess performed the twelve notable labors, as Gerion with three bodies, and as Cerberus with three heads, for I have slain three blown goat skins. But to the end that I may pardon thee of that which thou hast committed, perform the thing which I shall most earnestly desire of thee—that is, bring me that I may see and behold when thy mistress goes about any sorcery or enchantment, and when she prays to the gods, for I am very desirous to learn that art, and as it seems to me, thou thyself hast some experience in the same. For this I know and plainly feel that (whereas I have always irked and loathed the embracings and love of matrons) I am so stricken and subdued with thy shining eyes, ruddy cheeks, glittering hair, and lily-white bosom, that I have mind neither to go home nor to depart hence, but esteem the pleasure which I shall have with thee above all the joys of the world."

Then quoth she, "O my Lucius, how willing would I be to fulfill your desire, but by reason she is so hated, she gets herself into solitary places and out of the presence of every person when she minds to work her enchantment. Howbeit, I regard more to gratify your request than I esteem the danger of my life, and when I see opportunity and time I will assuredly bring you word, so that you shall see all her enchantment, but always upon this condition, that you secretly keep close such things as are done."

So she came to bed, and we passed the night in pastime and dalliance, till by drowsy sleep I was constrained to lie still.

*　　*　　*

THE DECEITS OF A WOMAN

There was a man dwelling in the town, very poor, who had nought but that which he got by the labor and travail of his hands. His wife was a fair young woman, but very lascivious and given to the appetite and desire of the flesh.

It fortuned on a day that while this poor man was gone betimes in the morning to the field about his business, according as he accustomed to do, his wife's lover secretly came into his house to have his pleasure with her. And so it chanced that during the time that he and she were busking together, her husband, suspecting no such matter, returned home, praising the chaste continency of his wife; and he found his doors fast closed, wherefore, as his custom was, he whistled to declare his coming home. Then his crafty wife, ready with present shifts, caught her lover and covered him under a great tub standing in a corner; and therewithal she opened the door, blaming her husband in this sort, "Comest thou home so every day with empty hands, and bringest nothing to maintain our house? Thou hast no regard for our profit, neither providest for any meat or drink, whereas I, poor wretch, do nothing day and night but occupy myself with spinning, and yet my travail will scarce find the candles which we spend. Oh, how much more happy is my neighbor Daphne, who eats and drinks at her pleasure, and passeth the time with her amorous lovers according to her desire."

"What is the matter?" (quoth her husband). "Though our master hath made holiday at the fields, yet think not but that I have made provision for our supper? Dost thou not see this tub that keeps a place here in our house in vain, and does us no service? Behold, I have sold it to a good fellow (that is here present) for fivepence. Wherefore I pray thee lend me thy hand that I may deliver him the tub."

His wife (having invented a present shift) laughed on her husband, saying, "What merchant, I pray you, have you brought home hither, to fetch away my tub for fivepence, for which I, poor woman that sit all day alone in my house, have been proffered so often seven?"

Her husband, being surprised at her words, demanded who he was that had bought the tub.

"Look" (quoth she), "he is gone under to see whether it be sound or no." Then her lover, under the tub, began to stir and rustle himself, and to the end that his words might agree to the words of the woman, he said, "Dame, will you have me tell the truth? This tub is rotten and cracked, as to me seemeth, on every side." And then he turned himself to her husband, saying, "I pray you, honest man, light a candle that I may make the tub clean within, to see if it be for my purpose or no, for I do not mind to cast away my money willfully."

He immediately (being a very ox) lighted a candle, saying, "I pray you, good brother, put not yourself to so much pain. Let me make the tub clean and ready for you." Whereupon he put off his coat and crept under the tub to rub away the filth from the sides. In the mean sea-son this minion lover had his pleasure with the wife, and as he was in the midst of his pastime he turned his head on this side and that side, finding fault with this and with that, till they had both ended their business, when he delivered sevenpence for the tub, and caused the good man himself to carry it on his back to his inn.

FROM

The Arabian Nights

Most of us grew up familiar with this classic work in its abridged form only; the most popular editions generally excise the following two passages—among many others.

Half of the fun of this work is the storytellers' objective: to keep the audience enthralled until dawn. Beware, though—having reached the goal, the tale-spinner will sometimes break off in the mid-plot. (See the titillatingly incomplete first excerpt for an example of this.)

Those who still think of this masterwork as a series of breathless adventure stories for young boys have almost certainly been deprived of a look at the work in its totality. It is an earthy, unendingly fascinating piece of work by mature storytellers for mature listeners.

✳ ✳ ✳

THE TWO HUNDRED AND SIXTH NIGHT

It hath reached me, O auspicious King, that when Kamar al-Zaman acquainted the Lady Budur with what he had seen in his dream, she and he went in to her sire and, telling him what had passed, besought his leave to travel. He gave the Prince the permission he sought; but the Princess said, "O my father, I cannot bear to be parted from him." Quoth Ghayur, her sire, "Then go thou with him," and gave her leave to be absent a whole twelve-month and afterwards to visit him in every year once; so she kissed his hand and Kamar al-Zaman did the like. Thereupon King Ghayur proceeded to equip his daughter and her bridegroom for the journey, and furnished them with outfit and appointments for the march; and brought out of his stables horses marked with his own brand, blood-dromedaries which can journey ten days without water, and prepared a litter for his daughter, besides load-ing mules and camels with victual; moreover, he gave them slaves and eunuchs to serve them and all manner of travelling gear; and on the day of departure, when King Ghayur took leave of Kamar al-Zaman, he bestowed on him ten splendid suits of cloth of gold embroidered with stones of price, together with ten riding horses and ten she-camels, and a treasury of money; and he charged him to love and cherish his daughter the Lady Budur. Then the King accompanied them to the farthest limits of his Islands where, going in to his daughter Budur in the litter, he kissed her and strained her to his bosom, weeping and repeating:

O thou who wooest Severance, easy fare! For love-embrace belongs to lover-friend:

Fare softly! Fortune's nature falsehood is, And part-ing shall love's every meeting end.

Then leaving his daughter, he went to her husband and bade him farewell and kissed him; after which he parted from them and, giving the order for the march he returned to his capital with his troops. The Prince and Princess and their suite fared on without stopping through the first day and the second and the third and the fourth; nor did they cease faring for a whole month till they came to a spacious champaign, abounding in pasturage, where they pitched their tents; and they ate and drank and rested, and the Princess Budur lay down to sleep. Presently, Kamar al-Zaman went in to her and found her lying asleep clad in a shift of apricot-coloured silk that showed all and everything; and on her head was a coif of gold-cloth embroidered with pearls and jewels. The breeze raised her shift which laid bare her navel and showed her breasts and displayed a stomach whiter than snow, each one of whose dimples would contain an ounce of benzoin- ointment. At this sight his love and longing redoubled, and he began reciting:

An were it asked me when by hell-fire burnt, When flames of heart my vitals hold and hem,

"Which wouldst thou chose, say wouldst thou rather them, Or drink sweet cooling draught?" I'd answer, "Them!"

Then he put his hand to the band of her petticoat-trousers and drew it and loosed it, for his soul lusted after her, when he saw a jewel, red as dye-wood, made fast to the band. He untied it and examined it and, seeing two lines of writing graven thereon, in a character not to be read, marvelled and said in his mind, "Were not this bezel something to her very dear she had not bound it to her trousers-band nor hidden it in the most privy and precious place about her person, that she might not be parted from it. Would I knew what she doth with this and what is the secret that is in it." So saying, he took it and went outside the tent to look at it in the light . . .

— And Shahrazad perceived the dawn of day, and ceased to say her permitted say.

* * *

THE RAKE'S TRICK AGAINST THE CHASTE WIFE
A certain man loved a beautiful and lovely woman, a model of charms and grace, married to a man whom she loved and who loved her. Moreover, she was virtuous and chaste, like unto me, and her rake of a lover found no way to her; so when his patience was at an end, he devised a device to win his will. Now the husband had a young man, whom he had brought up in his house and who was in high trust with him as his steward. So the rake addressed himself to the youth and ceased not insinuating himself into his favour by presents and fair words and deeds, til he became more obedient to him than the hand to the mouth and did whatever he ordered him. One day, he said to him, "Harkye, such an one; wilt thou not bring me into the family dwelling-place some time when the lady is gone out?" "Yes," answered the young steward; so, when his master was at the shop and his mistress gone forth to the Hammam, he took his friend by the hand and, bringing him into the house, showed him the sitting-rooms and all that was therein. Now the lover was determined to play a trick upon the woman; so he took the white of an egg which he had brought with him in a vessel, and spilt it on the merchant's bedding, unseen by the young man; after which he returned thanks and leaving the house went his way. In an hour or so the merchant came home; and, going to the bed to rest himself, found thereon something wet. So he took it up in his hand and looked at it and deemed it man's seed; whereat he stared at the young man with eyes of wrath, and asked him, "Where is thy mistress?"; and he answered, "She is gone forth to the Hammam and

will return forthright after she has made her ablutions."
When the man heard this, his suspicion concerning the
semen was confirmed; and he waxed furious and said,
"Go at once and bring her back." The steward accord-
ingly fetched her and when she came before her husband,
the jealous man sprang upon her and beat her a grievous
beating; then, binding her arms behind her, offered to cut
her throat with a knife; but she cried out to the neighbors,
who came to her, and she said to them, "This my man
hath beaten me unjustly and without cause and is minded
to kill me, though I know not what is mine offence." So
they rose up and asked him, "Why hast thou dealt thus by
her?" And he answered, "She is divorced." Quoth they,
"Thou hast no right to maltreat her; either divorce her or
use her kindly, for we know her prudence and purity and
chastity. Indeed, she hath been our neighbour this long
time and we wot no evil of her." Quoth he, "When I came
home, I found on my bed seed like human sperm, and I
know not the meaning of this." Upon this a little boy, one
of those present, came forward and said, "Show it to me,
nuncle mine!" When he saw it, he smelt it and, calling for
fire and a frying pan, he took the white of egg and cooked
it so that it became solid. Then he ate of it and made the
husband and others taste of it, and they were certified that
it was white of egg. So the husband was convinced that
he had sinned against his wife's innocence, she being
clear of all offence, and the neighbours made peace between them after the divorce, and he prayed her pardon
and presented her with an hundred gold pieces. And so
the wicked lover's cunning trick came to naught.

FROM

The Kama Sutra of Vatsyayana

Long suppressed in English-speaking countries to all but scholars, *The Kama Sutra* is a classic Hindu treatise on love. It deals not only with the categories and mechanics of lovemaking (which topic, to be sure, it treats in encyclopedic detail), but also on philosophy, class relations in an intricately class-conscious society, and the psychological relationship of the sexes. Central to any understanding of ancient India, the work is perhaps the most exhaustive and explicit examination of human sexuality to be found in the ancient world.

Sir Richard Burton completed his landmark translation of *The Kama Sutra* in 1838; his work was not widely available in America in anything like a mainstream edition until over a century later.

✳   ✳   ✳

(ON EMBRACES)

The embrace which indicates the mutual love of a man and woman who have come together is of four kinds:

Touching
Piercing
Rubbing
Pressing

The action in each case is denoted by the meaning of the word which stands for it.

1. When a man under some pretext or other goes in front of or alongside a woman and touches her body with his own, it is called the "touching embrace."

2. When a woman in a lonely place bends down, as if to pick up something, and pierces, as it were, a man sitting or standing, with her breasts, and the man in return takes hold of them, it is called a "piercing embrace."

These two embraces take place only between persons who do not, as yet, speak freely with each other.

3. When two lovers are walking slowly together, either in the dark or in a place of public resort, or in a lonely place, and rub their bodies against each other, it is called a "rubbing embrace."

4. When on the above occasion one of them presses the other's body forcibly against a wall or pillar, it is called a "pressing embrace."

These two last embraces are peculiar to those who know the intentions of each other.

At the times of meeting, the four following kinds of embrace are used:

Jataveshtitaka, or the twining of a creeper.

Vriskshadhirudhaka, or climbing a tree.

Tila-Tandulaka, or the mixture of sesame seed with rice.

Kshiraniraka, or milk-and-water embrace.

1. When a woman, clinging to a man as a creeper twines round a tree, bends his head down to hers with the desire of kissing him and slightly makes the sound of "*Sut, sut,*" embraces him, and looks lovingly toward him, it is called an embrace like the "twining of a creeper."

2. When a woman, having placed one of her feet on the foot of her lover, and the other on one of his thighs, passes one of her arms round his back, and the other on his shoulders, makes slightly the sounds of singing and cooing, and wishes, as it were to climb up him in order to have a kiss, it is called an embrace like the "climbing of a tree."

These two embraces take place when the lover is standing.

3. When lovers lie on a bed, and embrace each other so closely that the arms and thighs of one are encircled by the arms and thighs of the other, and are, as it were rubbing up against

them, this is called an embrace like "the mixture of sesame seed with rice."

4. When a man and a woman are very much in love with each other, and, not thinking of any pain or hurt, embrace each other as if they were entering into each other's bodies either while the woman is sitting on the lap of the man or in front of him, or on a bed, then it is called an embrace like a "mixture of milk and water."

These two embraces take place at the time of sexual union.

Babhravya has thus related to us the above eight kinds of embraces.

Suvarnanabha, moreover, gives us four ways of embracing simple members of the body, which are:

The embrace of the thighs.

The embrace of the *Jaghana*, that is, the part of the body from the navel downward to the thighs.

The embrace of the breasts.

The embrace of the forehead.

1. When one of two lovers presses forcibly one or both of the thighs of the other between his or her own, it is called the "embrace of thighs."

2. When the man presses the jaghana, or middle part, of the woman's body against his own, and mounts upon her to practice, either scratching with the nail or finger, or biting or striking or kissing, the hair of the woman being loose and flowing, it is called the "embrace of the jaghana."

3. When a man places his breast between the breasts of a woman and presses her with it, it is called the "embrace of the breasts."

4. When either of the lovers touches the mouth, the eyes, and the forehead of the other with his or her own, it is called the "embrace of the forehead."

Some say that even shampooing is a kind of embrace, because there is a touching of bodies in it. But Vatsyayana thinks that shampooing is performed at a different time, and for a different purpose; and as it is also of a different character, it cannot be said to be included in the embrace. There are also some verses on the subject, as follows:

"The whole subject of embracing is of such nature that men who ask questions about it, or who hear about it, or who talk about it, acquire thereby a desire for enjoyment. Even those embraces that are not mentioned in the *Kama Shastra* should be practiced at the time of sexual enjoyment, if they are in any way conducive to the increase of love or passion. The rules of the Shastra apply as long as the passion of man is middling, but when the wheel of love is once set in motion, there is then no Shastra and no order."

* * *

(ON THE WAYS OF LYING DOWN)

The Deer woman has the following three ways of lying down:

The widely opened position
The yawning position
The position of the wife of Indra

1. When she lowers her head and raises her middle parts, it is called the "widely opened position." At such a time the man should apply some unguent, so as to make the entrance easy.

2. When she raises her thighs and keeps them wide apart and engages in congress, it is called the "yawning position."

3. When she places her thighs with her legs doubled on them upon her sides, and thus engages in congress, it is called the position of Indrani, and this is learned only by practice. The position is also useful in the case of the "highest congress."

There are also the "clasping position" and the "low congress," and in the "lowest congress," together with the "pressing position," the "twining position" and the "mare's position."

When the legs of both the male and the female are stretched straight out over each other, it is called the "clasping position." It is of two kinds, the side position and the supine position, according to the way in which they lie down. In the side position the male should invariably lie on his left side, and cause the woman to lie on her right side, and this rule is to be observed in lying down with all kinds of women.

When, after congress has begun in the clasping position, the woman presses her lover with her thighs, it is called the "pressing position."

When the woman forcibly holds in her yoni the lingam after it is in, it is called the "mare's position." This is learned by practice only, and is chiefly found among the women of the Andra country.

The above are the different ways of lying down, mentioned by Babhravya; Suvarnanabha, however, gives the following in addition:

When the female raises both of her thighs straight up, it is called the "rising position."

When she raises both of her legs, and places them on her lover's shoulders, it is called the "yawning position."

When the legs are contracted, and thus held by the lover before his bosom, it is called the "pressed position."

When only one of her legs is stretched out, it is called the "half-pressed position."

When the woman places one of her legs on her lover's shoulder, and stretches the other out, and then places the latter on his shoulder, and stretches out the other, and continues to do so alternately, it is called the "splitting of a bamboo."

When one of her legs is placed on the head, and the other is stretched out, it is called the "fixing of a nail." This is learned by practice only.

When both the legs of the woman are contracted, and placed on her stomach, it is called the "crab's position."

When the thighs are raised and placed one upon the other, it is called the "packed position."

When the shanks are placed one upon the other, it is called the lotus-like position."

When a man, during congress, turns round, and enjoys the woman without leaving her, while she embraces him round the back all the time, it is called the "turning position," and is learned only by practice.

Thus, says Suvarnanabha, these different ways of lying down, sitting, and standing should be practiced in water, because it is easy to do so therein. But Vatsyayana is of opinion that congress in water is improper, because it is prohibited by the religious law.

When a man and a woman support themselves on each other's bodies, or on a wall or pillar, and thus while standing engage in congress, it is called the "supported congress."

When a man supports himself against a wall, and the woman, sitting on his hands joined together and held underneath her, throws her arms round his neck, and putting her thighs alongside his waist, moves herself by her feet, which are touching the wall against which the man is leaning, it is called the "suspended congress."

When a woman stands on her hands and feet like a quadruped, and her lover mounts her like a bull, it is called the "congress of a cow." At this time everything that is ordinarily done on the bosom should be done on the back.

In the same way can be carried on the congress of a dog, the congress of a goat, the congress of a deer, the forcible mounting of an ass, the congress of a cat, the jump of a tiger, the pressing of an elephant, the rubbing of a boar, and the mounting of a horse. And in all these cases the characteristics of the different animals should be manifested by acting like them.

When a man enjoys two women at the same time, both of whom love him equally, it is called the "united congress."

When a man enjoys many women altogether, it is called the "congress of a herd of cows."

The following kinds of congress, namely, sporting in water, or the congress of an elephant with many female elephants which is said to take place only in the water, the congress of a collection of goats, the congress of a collection of deer, take place in imitation of these animals.

In Gramaneri many young men enjoy a woman that may be married to one of them, either one after the other or at the same time. Thus one of them holds her, another enjoys her, a third uses her mouth, a fourth holds her middle part, and in this way they go on enjoying her several parts alternately.

The same thing can be done when several men are sitting in company with one courtesan, or when one courtesan is alone with many men. In the same way this can be done by the women of the king's harem when they accidentally get hold of a man.

The people in the Southern countries have also a congress in the anus, that is called the "lower congress."

＊　＊　＊

(ON WOMEN ACTING THE PART OF A MAN)

When a woman sees that her lover is fatigued by constant congress, without having his desire satisfied, she should, with his permission, lay him down upon his back, and give him assistance by acting his part. She may also do this to satisfy the curiosity of her lover, or her own desire of novelty.

There are two ways of doing this: the first is when during congress she turns round, and gets on top of her lover, in such a manner as to continue congress, without obstructing the pleasure of it; and the other is when she acts the man's part from the beginning. At such a time, with flowers in her hair hanging loose, and her smiles broken by hard breathings, she should press upon her lover's bosom with her own breasts; and, lowering her head frequently, she should do in return the same actions which he used to do before, returning his blows and chaffing him. She should say, "I was laid down by you, and fatigued with hard congress; I shall now therefore lay you down in return." She should then again manifest her own bashfulness, her fatigue, and her desire of stopping the congress. In this way she should do the work of a man, which we shall presently relate.

Whatever is done by a man for giving pleasure to a woman is called the work of a man, and is as follows:

While the woman is lying on his bed, and is as it were abstracted by his conversation, he should loosen the knot of her undergarments, and when she begins to dispute with him he should overwhelm her with kisses. Then when his lingham is erect he should touch her with his hands in various places, and gently manipulate various parts of the body. If the woman is bashful, and if it is the first time that they have come together, the man should place his hands between her thighs, which she would probably keep close together; and if she is a very young girl, he should first get his hands upon her breasts, which she would probably cover with her own hands, and under her armpits and on her neck. If, however, she is a seasoned woman, he should do whatever is agreeable either to him or to her, and whatever is fitting for the occasion. After this, he should take hold of her hair, and hold her chin in his fingers for the purpose of kissing her. On this, if she is a young girl, she will become bashful and close her eyes. In any event, he should gather from the action of the woman what things would be pleasing to her during congress.

Here Suvarnanabha says that while a man is doing to the woman what he likes best during congress, he should always make a point of pressing those parts of her body on which she turns her eyes.

The signs of the enjoyment and satisfaction of the woman are as follows: her body relaxes, she closes her eyes, she puts aside all bashfulness, and shows increased willingness to unite the two organs as closely together as possible. On the other hand, the signs of her want of enjoyment and of failing to be satisfied are as follows: she shakes her hands, she does not let the man get up, feels dejected, bites the man, kicks him, and continues to go on moving after the man has finished. In such cases the man should rub the yoni of the woman with his hand and fingers (as the elephant rubs anything with his trunk) before engaging in congress, until it is softened, and after that is done he should proceed to put his lingam into her.

The acts to be done by the man are:
Moving forward
Friction or churning
Piercing
Rubbing
Pressing
Giving a blow
The blow of a boar
The blow of a bull
The sporting of a sparrow

1. When the organs are brought together properly and directly, it is called "moving the organ forward."

2. When the lingam is held with the hand, and

turned all round in the yoni, it is called a "churning."

3. When the yoni is lowered, and the upper part of it is struck with the lingam, it is called "piercing."

4. When the same thing is done on the lower part of the yoni, it is called "rubbing."

5. When the yoni is pressed by the lingam for a long time, it is called "pressing."

6. When the lingam is removed to some distance from the yoni, and then forcibly strikes it, it is called "giving a blow."

7. When only one part of the yoni is rubbed with the lingam, it is called the "blow of a boar."

8. When both sides of the yoni are rubbed in this way, it is called the "blow of a bull."

9. When the lingam is in the yoni, and is moved up and down frequently, and without being taken out, it is called the "sporting of a sparrow." This takes place at the end of congress.

When a woman acts the part of a man, she has the following things to do in addition to the nine given above:
The pair of tongs
The top
The swing

1. When the woman holds the lingam in her yoni, draws it in, presses it, and keeps it thus in her for a long time, it is called the "pair of tongs."

2. When, while engaged in congress, she turns round like a wheel, it is called the "top." This is learned by practice only.

3. When, on such an occasion, the man lifts up the middle part of his body, and the woman turns round her middle part, it is called the "swing."

When the woman is tired, she should place her forehead on that of her lover, and should thus take rest without disturbing the union of the organs; and when the woman has rested herself the man should turn round and begin the congress again.

There are also some verses on the subject, as follows:

"Though a woman is reserved, and keeps her feelings concealed, yet when she gets on top a man, she then shows all her love and desire. A man should gather from the actions of the woman of what disposition she is, and in what way she likes to be enjoyed. A woman during her monthly courses, a woman who has been lately confined, and a fat woman should not be made to act the part of a man."

BOCCACCIO

The Decameron

Boccaccio's masterpiece is set against the fearsome
background of the plague years of fourteenth-century It-
aly. It is a colorful, robust series of stories that presages
Chaucer and Shakespeare in the breadth of its charac-
terization and the universality of its themes. The author's
cast of characters features a broad cross-section of the
society of the day: peasants, philosophers, tradesmen,
knights—and, here, an old and perhaps slightly too ambi-
tious judge.

This was one of the works nineteenth-century crusader Anthony Comstock felt was so dangerous that it
warranted legal penalties for anyone attempting to trans-
late it into English from the original Italian. He lobbied un-
successfully for legislation to that effect.

✳   ✳   ✳

There lived in Pisa a judge named Messer Riccardo
di Chinizica whose bad fortune it was to be endowed
more with intellectual than physical prowess. It may

have been his belief that a wife would be satisfied with the same type of work he brought to his research that led him to search out a beautiful young woman to marry . . . or, alternatively, it may have been his great wealth. Had he followed his own advice to others, however, he would have sought neither youth nor beauty!

His search ended successfully when Messer Lotto Gualindi offered his daughter Bartolomea, whose beauty was undeniably among the most exquisite in Pisa. Of course, it must be admitted that most of the women in Pisa resemble lizards.

The judge brought her home with great ceremony and, having held a spectacular wedding, took to the consummation. He lasted only one go-round with her—and barely made it that far, wizened and dried-up old thing that he was. The next morning he needed a shot or two of wine, some restorative confections, and any number of other props to make it back on his feet again.

Humbled now, and perhaps a better judge of his physical powers, he went about teaching his young wife the kind of calendar-sequence they may have used back at Ravenna. In short, he lied to her and presented to her many, many days in the year in which, he claimed, it is unholy for a man and wife to have intercourse. To these he added a ream of fast days, Emberdays, and vigils of the Apostles and innumerable other saints—not to mention all Fridays, all Saturdays, all Sundays, the whole of Lent, certain lunar phases, and a host of similar prohibited days. The result was that he acted under the assumption that one takes a holiday from sleeping with one's wife about as long as the recess between one's arguments in court.

And he was true to his word—much to the chagrin of his young wife, who was serviced once a month, if that. The old man took great pains to keep her from learning anything different about the calendar than what he had taught her.

[On a vacation trip, however, the couple is separated, and the wife is kidnaped by Paganin Da Mare, the most fearsome pirate of the day. The judge is inconsolable, but after some months manages to track down the pirate's lair. He offers ransom and demands her return, but the pirate answers, somewhat smirkingly, that he does not believe the woman will return to Pisa. The judge refuses to believe this, whereupon the two set off to put the question to Bartolomea directly. At the pirate's house, the judge is relieved to see his wife safe, and asks her to set the pirate straight and return home.]

Turning to Riccardo with the faintest smile on her face, she said, "Are you speaking to me, sir? Perhaps you have mistaken me for another. To the best of my knowledge, I have never laid eyes on you before."

"Come, come," said Riccardo. "Be careful of what you say. Look me over closely; if only you will try to recall, you will conclude without a shadow of a doubt that I am your very own Riccardo di Chinizica."

"Forgive me, sir," the lady replied, "for it may not be proper as you imagine for me to look at you at close range. Nevertheless, I can assure you that I have never seen you in my life."

[The judge persuades the pirate to leave the room and again begs his wife to show some sign of recognition, but at this she laughs long and loud.]

"You know very well," she said, "that I am not such an idiot that I do not realize you are Messer Riccardo di Chinizica, my husband. But while I lived with you, you proved that you hardly knew me at all. If you had half a brain, you would have seen that I was a young thing, still alive, and in need of that which young ladies require besides a meal and a set of clothes, even if, for reasons of modesty, they don't come out and say what they want. You yourself know how well you provided for that need.

"If the study of law meant more to you than a wife, then you should never have taken one! The fact is, though, you seemed to me less a judge and more a town crier calling out holy days, fasts, and vigils. You knew them all by heart!

"I am here to tell you, though, that if you gave as many holidays to the men who work your estates as you gave the fellow who was supposed to work this little field of mine right here, you'd never have harvested so much as a single grain of wheat!

"But as God—a compassionate onlooker to my youth—would please to have it, I came upon the man I share this room with. And here holidays are unknown. (I mean the kinds of holidays you observed so regularly, you who showed so much service to the heavens and so little service to women.) Not only have we kept the door discreetly shut here on Saturdays and Fridays and the vigils and the four days of Ember and Lent (Lent, which goes on until eternity!), but we also have at each other and thump our wool all day and all night!

"As a matter of fact, this very morning after matinsong was rung, I can assure you that my companion rose to the occasion to do a good deal of honest work right here where we speak!

"So I am planning to stay with him and get my work done while I'm young. And I'm going to put off all the saints' days and jubilees and fasts until I'm an old woman. You, sir, I advise to leave here post haste. I wish you the very best of luck. Celebrate every holiday in the calendar if you like. As for me, I am engaged in other business."

[The judge makes an impassioned plea to get her to return, and promises to treat her more to her liking. But he is greeted only with scorn:]

"Listen to this, my man: here, I am the wife of Paganino. In Pisa I played the whore, and had to memorize all the phases of the moon and calculate the quadratures of geometry necessary to bring the planets into conjunction before I got anywhere with you. Here Paganino holds me tightly in his arms the whole night through. He squeezes me; he bites me; and what else he does for me I will leave to the Almighty to set out plainly to you. You say you will try harder! What will that get me? Are you going to finish off in three strokes and then get it up again by smacking it?

"Who made you a bold, brave, knight since we last saw each other? Get out of here. Content yourself with continuing to draw breath. You're so peaked and wheeze so pathetically I'm sure you're still upright out of sheer force of habit.

"And let me go on: even if Paganino abandoned me (which he shows no sign of wanting to do as long as I remain here with him) I would never take it into my head to come back to you. And do you know why? Because I know that no matter how hard I squeezed, I'd never get so much as a half-teaspoonful of sauce out of you.

"I did stay with you once, and it was to my great loss that I did so. Now I will seek a better return elsewhere. I will tell you one more time: No. No more holidays. No more vigils. I am set on remaining here. Now in God's name, get out before I scream that you're trying to rape me."

CHAUCER

The Canterbury Tales

The first expurgated edition of Chaucer's unfinished four-teenth-century masterpiece *The Canterbury Tales* ap-peared in 1795; it was edited by an Oxford clergyman by the name of William Lipscomb. The passages that follow were all considerably shorter than you see them here by the time the Reverend Lipscomb had finished with them.

Lipscomb was the first in a long series of "purifiers" of this classic work of Middle English. *The Canterbury Tales* follows a group of pilgrims of many backgrounds on their way to Canterbury, England. The travelers engage in a tale-spinning contest to pass the time. Chaucer's characters—vivid, engaging personalities who tell re-markably diverse tales—occasionally take a startlingly frank approach to their subject matter.

Because modern English translations often leave one wondering exactly what has been omitted, we have chosen to stay with Chaucer's text and offer *[italicized]* help following the more difficult words and phrases.

✳   ✳   ✳

FROM *THE MILLER'S TALE*

When that the firste cok hat crowe *[cock had
        crowed]*, anoon
Up rist *[rises]* this joly lovere Absolon,
And him arrayeth gay at point devis *[at every point]*,
But first he cheweth grain and licoris *[cardamon
        and licorice]*,
To smellen sweete, er he hadded kembd his heer
        [before he'd combed his hair].
Under his tonge a trewe-love he beer *[sprig of mint
        he carried]*,
For thereby wende *[imagined]* he to be gracious
        [handsome].
He rometh *[saunters]* to the carpenteres hous,
And still he stant *[stands]* under the shot-windowe—
Unto his brest it raughte *[reached]*, it was so lowe—
And ofte he cougheth with a semisoun *[half a
        sound]*.
"What do ye, hony-comb, sweet Alisoun,
My faire brid *[bride]*, my sweete cinamome?
Awaketh, lemman *[mistress]* myn, and speketh to
        me . . . ."

*[But Alison, busy with her lover Nicholas, only insults
Absolon and orders him away from the window. Absolon,
ignorant of his rival's presence, refuses to leave unless
he receives a kiss from her.]*

"Woultou *[will you]* thann go thy way therwith?"
        quod *[said]* she.
"Ye, certes, *[Yes, surely]* lemman," quod this
        Absolon.
"Thanne meak thee redy," quod shee. "I come
        anoon."

And unto Nicholas she saide stille *[in a whisper]*,
"Now hust *[hush]*, and thou shalt laughen all thy
    fille."
This Absolon down sette him on his knees,
And said, "I am a lord at all degrees *[in every way]*,
For affter this I hope ther cometh more.
Lemman, thy grace, and sweete brid, thyn ore
    [favor]!"
The window she undooth, and that in haste.
"Have do," quod she, "com of and speed thee faste
    [hurry up],
Lest that our neighbors thee espye *[see]*."
This Absalon gan *[started to]* wype his mouth ful
    drye:
Derk was the night as pich *[pitch]* or as the cole
    [coal],
And at the window out she putte hir hole,
And Absolon, him fil no bet ne wers *[he did no
    better or worse]*,
But with his mouth he kiste hir naked ers *[ass]*
Ful savourly *[with gusto]*, er *[before]* he was war
    [aware] of this.
Abak he sterte, and thoghte it was amis,
For wel he wiste *[knew]* a womman hath no berd:
He felte a thing al rough and longe y-herd
    [longhaired],
And seyde, "Fy! allas! what have I do?" *[what have
    I done]*
"Tehee," quod she, and clapte the window to;
And Absolon goth forth a sory pas *[with sorry step]*.
"A berd, a berd!" quod hende *[handy]* Nicholas,
"By Goddes corpus *[God's body]*, this goth faire
    and weel."

This sely *[luckless]* Absolon herde every deel *[every word]*,
And on his lippe he gan for anger byte *[began to bite angrily]*,
And to himselfe he seyde, "I shall thee quyte!" *[I'll pay you back]*

✳   ✳   ✳

FROM *THE WIFE OF BATH'S TALE*
[The Wife of Bath recalls her techniques for dealing with husbands. She has had five, "three good and two bad."]

Of wenches wolde I beren hem on honde *[accuse them]*
What that for sik they mighte unnethe stonde *[When they were so sick they could hardly stand]*,
Yit tikled I his herte for *[because]* that he
Wende *[believed]* I hadded had of *[for]* him so greet cheertee *[fondness]*.
I swoor that al my walking out by nighte
Was for to espye *[spy on]* wenches that he dighte *[screwed]*.
Under that colour *[pretense]* had I many a mirthe.
For al swich *[such]* wit is yiven *[given]* us in our birthe:
Deciete, weeping, spinning God hath yive *[given]*
To wommen kindely whil they may live.
And thus of oo *[one]* thing I avaunte me *[boast]*:
At ende I hadde the bet *[advantage]* in eeche degree *[every case]*,

By sleighte *[trick]* or force, or by som manere
    [similar] thing,
As by continuel murmur *[complaining]* or
    grucching *[grouching]*;
Namely abbede *[Especially if in bed]* hadden they
    mischaunce *[mishaps]*:
There wolde I chide and do hem no plesaunce
    [favors];
I wolde no lenger *[longer]* in the bed abide
If that I felte his arm over my side,
Tiil he had maad his ranson *[ransom]* unto me;
Thanne wolde I suffre *[let]* him do his nicetee
    [business].
And therfore every man this tale I telle:
Winne whoso *[whoever]* may, for all is for to selle;
With empty hand men may no hawkes lure.
For winning *[profit]* wolde I al his lust endure,
And make me a feined *[pretended]* appetit—
And yit *[yet]* in bacon *[old meat]* hadde I nevere
    delit *[delight]*.
That made me that evere *[That's why]* I wolde hem
    [them] chide;
For though *[even if]* the Pope had seten hem biside
    [sitting next to them],
I wolde nought spare hem *[them]* at hir *[their]*
    owene boord *[household]*.
For by my trouth, I quitte hem *[repaid them]* word
    for word.
As help me verray God omnipotent, *[So help me
    almighty God]*
Though I right now sholde make my testament,
I ne owe hem nat a word that it nis quit. *[I owe
    them not a word that isn't paid]*
I broughte it so aboute by my wit

That they moste yive it up *[give up]* as for the beste,
Or elles hadd we nvere been in reste *[had any
    peace]*;
For though he looked as a wood leoun *[angry lion]*,
Yet sholde he fail of his conclusion *[lose the
    argument]*.
Thanne wolde I say, "Goodelief taak keep, *[Honey,
    look]*
How mekely *[gentle]* looketh Wilekin, oure sheep!
Com neer, my spouse, lat me ba *[kiss]* thy cheeke—
Ye sholden *[should]* be al patient and meeke,
And han a sweete-spiced *[pleasing]* conscience,
Sith ye so precehe *[Since you preach so]* of Jobes
    pacience;
Suffreth alway *[Always be patient]*, sin *[since]* ye so
    wel can prech;
And but *[unless]* ye do, certain, we shal you teche
That it is fair *[good]* to han *[have]* a wif in pees
    [peace].
Oon *[One]* of us two moste bowen *[must bend]*,
    douteless,
And sith *[since]* a man is more resonable
Than womman is, ye mosten been suffrable
    [patient].
What aileth you to grucche *[grouch]* thus and grone?
Is it for *[because]* ye wold have my queinte *[cunt]*
    allone?
Why taak it al—lo, have it, everydeel *[every inch]*.
Peter, I shrewe *[curse]* you but ye love it weel.
For if I wolde sell my bele chose *[fair little thing]*,
I coude walke as fressh as is a rose;
But I wol keep it for youre owene tooth *[tastes]*.
Ye be to blame. By God, I say you sooth!" *[tell you
    truly]*

* * *

[The Wife of Bath recalls her fourth and fifth husbands.]
But Lord Crist, whan that it remembreth me *[when I
think back]*
Upon my youthe and on my jolitee,
It tikleth me aboute myn herte roote— *[to the
depths of my heart]*
Unto this day it dooth myn herte boote *[good]*
That I have had my world as in my time.
But age, allas, that al wol envenime *[that destroys
everything]*,
Hath me biraft *[Has taken from me]* my beautee and
my pith—
Lat *[let it]* go, farewel, the devel go therwith *[with
it]*!
The flour is goon *[gone]*, ther is namore *[no more]*
to telle:
The bren *[bran]* as I best can now moste *[must]* I
selle;
But yit *[yet]* to be right merye wol I fonde *[try]*.
Now wol I tellen *[tell]* of my ferthe *[fourth]*
housbonde.

I saye I hadde in herte greet despit *[great anger]*
That he of any other had delit,
But he was quit *[repaid]*, by God and by Saint Joce:
I made him of the same wode a croce— *[I made a
cross for him of the same wood]*
Nat of *[Not with]* my body in no foul manere—
But, certainly, I made folk swich cheere *[such
merriment with men]*
That in his owene grece *[grease]* I made him frye,

For angre and for verray *[true]* jalousye.
By God, in *[on]* erthe I was his purgatorye,
For which I hope his soule be in glorye.
For God it woot *[God knows]*, he sat ful ofte and
    soong *[sang out]*
Whan that his sho ful bitterly him wroong *[his shoe
    pinched him tight]*.
There was no wight save God and he that wiste
    [None but he and God know]
In many wise how sore I him twiste. *[How terribly I
    treated him]*
He deide whan I cam from Jerusalem,
And lith ygrave *[lies buried]* under the roode
    beem— *[crucifix beam]*
Al is his tombe nought so curious *[Although his
    tomb is not so well made]*
As was the sepulcre of him Darius *[Darius (a
    legendary medieval king)]*,
Which that Apelles wroughte subtilly *[made so
    skilfully]*:
It nis but wast *[would have been a waste]* to burye
    him preciously *[extravagantly]*.
Lat *[Let]* him fare wel, God yive *[give]* his soule
    reste;
He is now in his grave and in his cheste *[coffin]*.
Now of my fifth housbonde wol *[will]* I telle—
God lete his soule never come in helle—
And yit *[yet]* he was to me the moste shreww
    [cruel]:
That feele I *[I can feel that]* on my ribbes al by
    rewe *[row]*,
And evere shal unto myn ending day.
But in oure bed he was so fressh and gay,

And therwithal so wel coulde he me glose
    [manipulate]
What that he wolde han my bele chose, *[Whenever*
    he would go to work on my crotch]
That though he hadde be bet on every boon, *[Even*
    if he had beaten my every bone]
He could winne again my love annon *[soon]* . . .

Now wol I tellen forth what happed *[happened to]*
    me.
I saye that in the feeldes walked we, *[I walked in*
    the fields (with my future husband)]
Til trewely we hadde such daliaunce *[flirtations]*,
This clerk and I, that, of my purveyaunce *[thinking*
    ahead],
I spake to him and saide how that he,
If I were widowe, sholde wedde me.
For certainly, I saye for no bobuance *[without*
    boasting],
Yet I was never withouten purveyaunce *[foresight]*
Of marriage n'of *[and of]* of othere thinges eek *[as*
    well].
I holde a mouses herte *[mouse's heart]* nought
    worth a leek
That hath but oon *[one]* hole for to sterte *[run]* to,
And *[For]* if that faile, thanne is all ydo *[lost]*.
I bar him on hand *[I led him to believe]* he hadde
    enchanted me
(My dame *[mother]* taughte me that subtiltee);
And eek *[also]* I saide I mette *[dreamed]* of him al
    night:
He wolde han slain me as I lay upright,

*[(I dreamed) that he wanted to slay me as I lay
upon my back]*
And al my bed was ful of verray *[real-looking]*
blood—
"But yit *[yet]* I hope that ye shul *[shall]* do me good;
For blood bitokenoth gold *[Since blood in dreams
means gold]*, as me was taught."
And al was fals *[Every word was false]*, I dremed of
it right naught,
But as I folwed ay my dames lore *[followed my
mother's teaching]*
As wel of that as *[In that matter as in]* other thinges
more . . . .

Whan that my ferthe housbonde was on beere
[taken to burial],
I weep algate *[I wept false tears]*, and made sory
cheere,
As wives moten *[must]*, for it is usage *[expected]*,
And with my coverchief covered my visage;
But for I was purveyed of a make *[But since I had a
husband lined up]*
I wept but smale *[little]*, and that I undertake
[promise].
To chirche was myn housbonde born amorwe
[carried in the morning],
With neighbores that for him maden sorowe,
And Jankekin our clerk was oon of tho *[one of
them]*.
As *[So]* help me God, whan that I saw him go
After the beere *[behind the procession]*, me thought
he had a paire
Of legges and of feet so clene *[neat]* and faire,

That al myn herte I yaf *[gave]* unto his hold
     [possession].
He was, I trowe *[think]*, twenty winter old,
And I was fourty, if I shal saye sooth *[truly]*—
But yit I hadde alway a coltes tooth: *[But I always
     had a taste for the things of youth]*
Gat-toothed *[Horny]* was I, and that bicam me weel
     [well];
I hadde the prente of Sainte Venues seel. *[I carried
     the seal of Saint Venus]*
As *[So]* help me God, I was a lusty oon *[one]*,
And fair and riche and wel-bigoon *[well provided
     for]*,
And trewely, as mine housbondes tolde me,
I hadde the best quoniam mighte be. *[I had the best
     twat imaginable]*

Dr. Bowdler and the Bard

Dr. Thomas Bowdler's nineteenth-century bestseller *The Family Shakespeare* was a defining work of the times. Recalling his own childhood experiences in the Introduction, Bowdler praised his father's deft omission of "words and expressions improper to be pronounced" in family readings of the Bard's works; the good doctor carried on the family tradition in his enormously popular version of the "complete" works of Shakespeare.

The book was praised by the critics of the day; one blunt rave review notes that "all admirers of Shakespeare must be aware that such a castrated version of his plays has long been desirable." Bowdler's relentless pruning-away of sexual references, oaths, and even the most mildly suggestive metaphors came to symbolize Victorian prudery at its zenith. *The Family Shakespeare* also eventually produced a new verb, "to bowdlerize," which the *Random House Dictionary of the English Language* defines as "to expurgate by removing or modifying passages considered vulgar." ("By the bowdlerizer," one is tempted to add.)

There follow some of the more notable passages that ran afoul of Dr. Bowdler's sensibilities.

* * *

THE "PRICK" PROBLEM

These speeches of Mercutio's and Touchstone's apparently rubbed Dr. Bowdler the wrong way.

NURSE: God ye good morrow, gentlemen.
MERCUTIO: God ye good den [afternoon], fair gentlewoman.
NURSE: Is it good den?
MERCUTIO: 'Tis no less, I tell you; for the bawdy hand of the dial is now upon the prick of noon.
NURSE: Out upon you! What a man are you!
— *Romeo and Juliet*, II, iv

TOUCHSTONE: Winter garments must be lined,
So must slender Rosalind.
They that reap must sheaf and bind,
Then to cart with Rosalind.
Sweetest nut hath sourest rind,
Such a nut is Rosalind.
He that sweetest rose will find
Must find love's prick and Rosalind.
— *As You Like It*, III, ii

* * *

THE "LAP" PROBLEM

One of the seventeenth-century meanings of the word "lap" was a ribald one relating to the female genitals. It's not entirely clear whether Bowdler was aware of the double meaning, but he did deny Shakespeare the clearly sexual references in the following passages:

HAMLET: Lady, shall I lie in your lap?
OPHELIA: No, my lord.
HAMLET: I mean, my head upon your lap?
OPHELIA: Ay, my lord.
HAMLET: Do you think I meant country matters?
OPHELIA: I think nothing, my lord.
HAMLET: That's a fair thought to lie between maids' legs.
OPHELIA: What is, my lord?
HAMLET: Nothing.
OPHELIA: You are merry, my lord.
— *Hamlet*, III, ii

ROMEO: . . . She'll not be hit
With Cupid's arrow; she hath Dian's wit;
And, in strong proof of chastity well arm'd,
From love's weak childish bow she lives unharm'd.
She will not stay the siege of loving terms,
Nor bide the encounter of assailing eyes,
Nor ope her lap to saint-seducing gold.
— *Romeo and Juliet*, I, i

*　*　*

THE GEOGRAPHY PROBLEM

The following lighthearted passage might have been justified on the grounds that it yields a memorable lesson in the relative positioning of the world's nations. Bowdler apparently felt otherwise, and took a dim view of the topographical details the Bard provided on Ireland, England, Belgium and the Netherlands.

DROMIO OF SYRACUSE: She is spherical, like a globe, I could find out countries in her.

ANTONIO OF SYRACUSE: In what part of her body stands Ireland?

DROMIO OF SYRACUSE: Marry, sir, in her buttocks; I found it out by the bogs.

ANTONIO OF SYRACUSE: Where Scotland?

DROMIO OF SYRACUSE: I found it by the barrenness; hard in the palm of the hand.

ANTONIO OF SYRACUSE: Where France?

DROMIO OF SYRACUSE: In her forehead; armed and reverted, making war against her heir.

ANTONIO OF SYRACUSE: Where England?

DROMIO OF SYRACUSE: I looked for the chalky cliffs, but I could find no whiteness in them: but I guess it stood in her chin, by the salt rheum that ran between France and it.

ANTONIO OF SYRACUSE: Where Spain?

DROMIO OF SYRACUSE: Faith, I saw not: but I felt it hot in her breath.

ANTONIO OF SYRACUSE: Where America, the Indies?

DROMIO OF SYRACUSE: Oh, sir upon her nose, all o'er embellished with rubies, carbuncles, sapphires, declining their rich aspect to the hot breath of Spain, who sent armadoes of caracks to be ballast at her nose.

ANTONIO OF SYRACUSE: Where stood Belgia, the Netherlands?

DROMIO OF SYRACUSE: Oh, sir, I did not look so low.
— *The Comedy of Errors*, III, ii

FROM

The King James Translation of the Bible

Sex in the Bible has, if not a history of suppression, a history of intentional misinterpretation. Elizabeth Bowdler, the mother of Thomas Bowdler, the famed expurgator of Shakespeare, produced a remarkably lifeless paraphrase and commentary of the Song of Solomon. She argued that the translation of the first excerpt we feature below had to have been in error. Her logic: that a grown man was   too large to actually fit "betwixt" his wife's breasts. Mrs. Bowdler also changed all the Bride's references to her conjugal "bed" to the more decorous "bridal chariot."

Similar nibblings-away at explicit passages were not uncommon. John Watson, editor of *The Holy Bible Arranged and Adapted for Family Reading*, wasn't content with revisions. He excised the section from Genesis we reproduce here, and refused to print a line of the Song of Solomon.

✳   ✳   ✳

A bundle of myrrh is my well-beloved unto me; he shall lie all night betwixt my breasts. My beloved is unto me as a cluster of camphire in the vineyards of Engedi.
— *The Song of Solomon* 1:13-14

My beloved is white and ruddy, the chiefest among ten thousand. His head is as the most fine gold; his locks are bushy, and black as a raven. His eyes are as the eyes of doves by the rivers of waters, washed with milk, and fitly set: His cheeks are as a bed of spices, as sweet flowers: his lips like lilies, dropping sweet smelling myrrh: His hands are as gold rings set with the beryl: his belly is as bright ivory overlaid with sapphires: His legs are as pillars of marble, set upon sockets of fine gold: his countenance is as Lebanon, excellent as the cedars: His mouth is most sweet: yea, he is altogether lovely. This is my beloved, and this is my friend, O daughters of Jerusalem.
— *The Song of Solomon* 5:10-16

How beautiful are thy feet with shoes, O prince's daughter! The joints of thy thighs are like jewels, the work of the hands of a cunning workman. Thy navel is like a round goblet, which wanteth not liquor: thy belly is like a heap of wheat set about with lilies. Thy two breasts are like two young roes that are twins. Thy neck is as a tower of ivory; thine eyes like the fishpools in Heshbon, by the gate of Bathrabbim: thy nose is as the tower of Lebanon which looketh toward Damascus. Thine head upon thee is like Carmel, and the hair of thine head like purple: the King is held in the galleries. How fair and how pleasant art thou, O love, for delights! This thy stature is like to a palm tree, and thy breasts to clusters of grapes. I said, I will go up to the palm tree, I will take hold of the boughs thereof: now also thy breasts shall be as clusters of the vine, and the smell of thy nose like apples; And the roof of thy mouth like the best wine for my beloved, that goeth down sweetly, causing the lips of those that are asleep to speak.

— *The Song of Solomon* 7:1-9

And Lot went up out of Zoar, and dwelt in the mountain, and his two daughters with him; for he feared to dwell in Zoar: and he dwelt in a cave, he and his two daughters. And the first born said unto the younger, Our father is old, and there is not a man in the earth to come in unto us after the manner of all the earth: Come, let us make our father drink wine, and we will lie with him, that we may preserve seed of our father. And they made their father drink wine that night: and the first born went in, and lay with her father; and he perceived not when she lay down, nor when she arose. And it came to pass on the morrow, that the first born said unto the younger, Behold, I lay yesternight with my father: let us make him drink wine this night also; and go thou in, and lie with him, that we may preserve seed of our father. And they made their father drink wine that night also: and the younger arose, and lay with him; and he perceived not when she lay down, nor when she arose. Thus were both the daughters of Lot with child by their father. And the first born bare a son, and called his name Moab: the same is the father of the Moabites unto this day. And the younger, she also

bare a son, and called his name Benammi: the same is the father of the children of Ammon unto this day.
— *Genesis* 19:30-38

JOHN DONNE

To His Mistress Going to Bed

There were for decades two competing types of "complete" editions of John Donne's works; inexpensive ones, widely distributed, that silently passed over the poet's earthier works, and expensive ones available only to scholars that included everything. The wealthier the reader, presumably, the less discretion is necessary on the part of the editor.

One of Donne's most heartfelt and moving poems was also among the most commonly excluded; it is still difficult to find it in some of the older volumes.

✳ ✳ ✳

Come; Madam, come, all rest my powers defy,
Until I labour, I in labour lie.
The foe oft-times, having the foe in sight,
Is tired with standing, though they never fight.
Off with that girdle, like heaven's zone glistering,

But a far fairer world encompassing.
Unpin that spangled breastplate which you wear,
That th'eyes of busy fools may be stopped there:
Unlace yourself, for that harmonious chime.
Tells me from you that now it's your bed time.
Off with that happy busk, which I envy,
That still can be, and still can stand so nigh.
Your gown's going off, such beauteous state reveals,
As when from flowery meads th'hill's shadow steals.

     Off with your wiry coronet and show
The hairy diadem which on you doth grow.
Off with those shoes and then safely tread
In this love's hallowed temple, this soft bed.
In such white robes, heaven's angels used to be
Received by men; thou Angel bring'st with thee
A heaven like Mahomet's Paradise; and though
Ill spirits walk in white, we easily know,
By this these Angels from an evil sprite;
They set our hairs, but these the flesh upright.

     Licence my roving hands, and let them go,
Behind, before, above, between, below.
Oh my America! my new found-land,
My kingdom, safeliest when with one man manned,
My mine of precious stones, my Empery,
How blessed am I in this discovering thee!
To enter in these bonds is to be free
Then where my hand is set my seal shall be.

     Full nakedness, all joys are due to thee,
As souls unbodied, bodies unclothed must be
To taste whole joys. Gems which you women use
Are as Atlanta's balls, cast in men's views,
That when a fool's eye lighteth on a gem,
His earthly soul may covet theirs not them.
Like pictures, or like books' gay coverings made

For lay-men, are all women thus arrayed;
Themselves are mystic books, which only we
Whom their imputed grace will dignify
Must see revealed. Then since that I may know,
As liberally as to a midwife show
Thyself, cast all, yea this white linen hence.
Here is no penance, much less innocence.

     To teach thee, I am naked first. Why then
What need'st thou have more covering than a man.

ROBERT HERRICK

Hesperides

This mid-seventeenth century poet, much admired by Edwardians and Victorians supplied with watered-down editions, had an earthier side than many of his later readers imagined. His editors knew, of course, but they were, for the most part, content to omit or rewrite Herrick with a free hand. "Much that was admissible centuries since," one of them explains patiently, "or at least sought admission, has now, by a law against which protest is idle, lapsed into the indecorous."

At the risk of protesting against the laws governing the regulation of the indecorous, here are some classic bursts of suppressed Herrick.

❋   ❋   ❋

TO HIS MISTRESSES
    Help me! help me! now I call
    To my pretty witchcrafts all;
    Old I am, and cannot do
    That I was accustomed to.

Bring your magics, spells, and charms,
To enflesh my thighs and arms;
Is there no way to beget
In my limbs their former heat?
Aeson had, as poets feign,
Baths that made him young again:
Find that medicine, if you can,
For your dry, decrepit man
Who would fain his strength renew,
Were it but to pleasure you.

* * *

UPON JULIA'S FALL

Julia was careless, and withal
She rather took than got a fall;
The wanton ambler chanc'd to see
Part of her legs' sincerity:
And ravish'd thus, it came to pass,
The nag (like to the prophet's ass)
Began to speak, and would have been
A-telling what rare sights he'd seen:
And had told all; but did refrain
Because his tongue was tied again.

* * *

THE VISION

Sitting alone, as one forsook,
Close by a silver-shedding brook,
With hands held up to love, I wept;
And after sorrows spent I slept;
Then in a vision I did see
A glorious form appear to me:
A virgin's face she had; her dress
Was like a sprightly Spartaness.
A silver bow, with green silk strung,
Down from her comely shoulders hung:
And as she stood, the wanton air
Dangled the ringlets of her hair.
Her legs were such Diana shows
When, tucked up, she a-hunting goes;
With buskins shortened to descry
The happy dawning of her thigh:
Which when I saw, I made access
To kiss that tempting nakedness:
But she forbade me with a wand
Of myrtle she had in her hand:
And, chiding me, said: Hence, remove,
Herrick, thou art too coarse to love.

The Earl of Rochester's Diversions

John Wilmot, Earl of Rochester's case is an interesting one.

Some of this seventeenth-century English noble's poems were, shortly after his death, printed in a prim and popular edition noting that the contents were fit "to be re-ceiv'd in a vertuous Court." This was to distinguish them from the dozens of erotic works of Rochester's that had been circulated underground for some time. Rochester's literary career has thus proceeded on two fronts since his death, one suppressed and one "legitimate." Here are a few of the notable poems from Lord Rochester's "other" literary career.

* * *

THE IMPERFECT ENJOYMENT

Naked she lay, clasped in my longing arms,
I filled with love, and she all over charms;
Both equally inspired with eager fire,
Melting through kindness, flaming in desire.
With arms, legs, lips close clinging to embrace,
She clips me to her breast, and sucks me to her face.
Her nimble tongue, Love's lesser lightning, played
Within my mouth, and to my thoughts conveyed
Swift orders that I should prepare to throw
The all-dissolving thunderbolt below.
My fluttering soul, sprung with the pointed kiss,
Hangs hovering o'er her balmy brinks of bliss.
But whilst her busy hand would guide that part
Which should convey my soul up to her heart,
In liquid raptures I dissolve all o'er,
Melt into sperm, and spend at every pore.
A touch from any part of her had done't:
Her hand, her foot, her very look's a cunt.

Smiling, she chides in a kind murmuring noise,
And from her body wipes the clammy joys,
When, with a thousand kisses wandering o'er
My panting bosom, "Is there then no more?"
She cries. "All this to love and rapture's due;
Must we not pay a debt to pleasure too?"

But I, the most forlorn, lost man alive,
To show my wished obedience vainly strive:
I sigh, alas! and kiss, but cannot swive.
Eager desires confound my first intent,
Succeeding shame does more success prevent,
And rage at last confirms me impotent.
Ev'n her fair hand, which might bid heat return
To frozen age, and make cold hermits burn,
Applied to my dead cinder, warms no more

Than fire to ashes could past flames restore.
Trembling, confused, despairing, limber, dry,
A wishing, weak, unmoving lump I lie.
This dart of love, whose piercing point, oft tried,
With virgin blood ten thousand maids have dyed;
Which nature still directed with such art
That it through every cunt reached every heart—
Stiffly resolved, 'twould carelessly invade
Woman or man, nor ought its fury stayed:
Where'er it pierced, a cunt it found or made—
Now languid lies in this unhappy hour,
Shrunk up and sapless like a withered flower.

      Thou treacherous, base deserter of my flame,
False to my passion, fatal to my fame,
Through what mistaken magic dost thou prove
So true to lewdness, so untrue to love?
What oyster-cinder-begger-common whore
Didst thou e'er fail in all thy life before?
When vice, disease, and scandal lead the way,
With what officious haste dost thou obey!
Like a rude, roaring hector in the streets
Who scuffles, cuffs, and justles all he meets,
But if his King or country claim his aid,
The rakehell villain shrinks and hides his head;
Ev'n so thy brutal valor is displayed,
Breaks every stew, does each small whore ivade,
But when great Love the onset does command,
Base recreant to thy prince, thou dar'st not stand.
Worst part of me, and henceforth hated most,
Through all the town a common fucking post,
On whom each whore relieves her tingling cunt
As hogs on gates do rub themselves and grunt,
Mayst thou to ravenous chancres be a prey,
Or in consuming weepings waste away;

May strangury and stone thy days attend;
May'st thou ne'er piss, who didst refuse to spend
When all my joys did on false thee depend.
    And may ten thousand abler pricks agree
    To do the wronged Corinna right for thee.

✳ ✳ ✳

UPON HIS LEAVING HIS MISTRESS
'Tis not that I am weary grown
Of being yours, and yours alone;
But with what face can I incline
To damn you to be only mine?
    You, whom some kinder power did fashion,
    By merit and by inclination,
    The joy at least of one whole nation.

Let meaner spirits of your sex
With humbler aims their thoughts perplex,
And boast if by their arts they can
Contrive to make one happy man;
    Whilst, moved by an impartial sense,
    Favors like nature you dispense
    With universal influence.

See, the kind seed-receiving earth
To every grain affords a birth.
On her no showers unwelcome fall;
Her willing womb retains 'em all.
    And shall my Celia be confined?
    No! Live up to thy mighty mind,
    And be the mistress of mankind.

SIR CHARLES SEDLEY

The Fall

Some authors are expurgated or bowdlerized; others are consigned to oblivion for a century or two. Sir Charles Sedley falls into the latter category; no publisher saw fit to publish an edition of his poems for the whole of the nineteenth century.

The Fall takes the same theme of Robert Herrick's Upon Julia's Fall—and adds a scornful reproof from the watched to the watcher.

* * *

As Chloe o'er the meadows past
        I viewed the lovely maid:
She turned and blushed, renewed her haste,
And feared by me to be embraced—
        My eyes my wish betrayed.

I trembling felt the rising flame,
        The charming nymph pursued;
Daphne was not so bright a game,

Tho' great Apollo's darling dame,
        Nor with such charms endued.

I followed close, the fair still flew
        Along the grassy plain;
The grass at length my rival grew,
And catched my Chloe by the shoe;
        Her speed was then in vain.

But, oh! as tottering down she fell,
        What did the fall reveal?
Such limbs descriptions cannot tell;
Such charms were never in the Mall,
        Nor smack did e'er conceal.

She shrieked; I turned my ravished eyes
        And, burning with desire,
I helped the Queen of Love to rise;
She checked her anger and surprise,
        And said, "Rash youth, retire,

"Begone, and boast what you have seen;
        It shan't avail you much:
I know you like my form and mien,
Yet since so insolent you've been,
        The Parts disclosed you ne'er shall touch."

MATTHEW PRIOR

Nanny Blushes, When I Woo Her

Editor Austin Dobson produced a bowdlerized edition of the works of this eighteenth-century English poet. In defense of his numerous cuts and changes—typically unannotated—Dobson wrote, "I trust I shall be acquitted of the impertinence of improving Prior." Here, unimproved, is one of Prior's unapologetically exuberant works.

✳   ✳   ✳

Nanny blushes, when I woo her,
And with kindly chiding eyes,
Faintly says, I shall undoe her,
Faintly, O forbear, she cries.

But her Breasts while I am pressing,
While to hers my Lips I joyn;
Warm'd she seems to taste the Blessing,
And her kisses answer mine.

Undebauch'd by Rules of Honour,
Innocence, with nature, charms;
One bids, gently push me from her,
T'other, take me in her Arms.

ALEXANDER POPE

Sober Advice from Horace, to the Young Gentleman About Town

It is estimated that approximately fifty published editions purporting to be all-inclusive collections of Pope's work excluded the following poem. Of it, one of Pope's editors wrote curtly, "The offensive epistle is excluded," and left the matter at that. Many of the editors were not even this honest, arguing that Pope had simply not written the piece.

Write it he did, although he left a lot of blank spots when referring to powerful people and particularly spicy phrases. This was a common practice of the day, a kind of self-censorship. In Pope's case, it simply didn't go far enough to suit his later editors.

✳   ✳   ✳

The Tribe of Templars, Play'rs, Apothecaries,
Pimps, Poets, Wits, Lord Fanny's, Lady Mary's,
And all the Court in Tears, and half the Town,
Lament dear charming Oldfield, dead and gone!
Engaging Oldfield! Who, with Grace and Ease,
Could joyn the Arts, to ruin, and to please.

    Not so, who of Ten Thousand gull'd her Knight,
Then ask'd Ten Thousand for a second Night:
The Gallant too, to whom she pay'd it down,
Liv'd to refuse that Mistress half a Crown.

    Con Philips cries, 'A sneaking Dog I hate.'
That's all three Lovers have for their Estate!
'Treat on, treat on,' is her eternal Note,
And Lands and Tenements go down her Throat.
Some damn the Jade, and some the Cullies blame,
But not Sir H—t, for he does the same.

    With all a Woman's Virtues but the P—x,
Fufidia thrives in Money, Land, and Stocks:
For Int'rest, ten *per Cent* Her constant Rate is;
Her Body? Hopeful Heirs may have it *gratis*.
She turns her very sister to a Job,
And, in the Happy Minute, picks your Fob:
Yet starves herself, so little her own Friend,
And thirsts and hungers only at one End:
A Self-Tormentor, worse than (in the Play)
The Wretch, whose Av'rice drove his *Son* away.

    But why all this? I'll tell ye, 'tis my Theme:
'Women and Fools are always in Extreme.'
Rufa's at either end a Common-Shoar,
Sweet *Moll* and *Jack* are Civet-Cat and Boar:
Nothing in Nature is so lewd as Peg,
Yet, for the world, she would not shew her Leg!
While bashful *Jenny*, ev'n at Morning-Prayer,
Spreads her Fore-Buttocks to the Navel bare.

But diff'rent Taste in diff'rent Men prevails,
And one is fired by Heads, and one by Tails;
Some feel no Flames but at the *Court* or *Ball*,
And others hunt white Aprons in the *Mall*.
  My lord of L—n, chancing to remark
A *noted Dean* much busy'd in the Park,
'Proceed (he cry'd) proceed, my Reverend Brother,
'Tis *Fornicatio simplex*, and no other:
Better than lust for Boys, with *Pope* and *Turk*,
Or others' Spouses, like my Lord of —'
  May no such Praise (cries *J—s*) e'er be mine!
J—s, who bows at *Hi—sb—w's hoary Shrine*.
All you, who think the City ne'er can thrive,
Till ev'ry Cuckold-maker's flea'd alive;
Attend, while I their Miseries explain,
And pity Men of Pleasure still in Pain!
Survey the Pangs they bear, the Risques they run,
Where the most lucky are but last undone.
See wretched *Monsieur* flies to save his Throat,
And quits his Mistress, Money, Ring, and Note!
See good Sir *George* of ragged Livery stript,
By worthier Footmen pist upon and whipt!
Plunder'd by Thieves, or Lawyers which is worse,
One bleeds in Person, and one bleeds in Purse;
This meets a Blanket, and that meets a Cudgel—
And all applaud the Justice—All, but *Budgel*.
  How much more safe, dear Countrymen! his State,
Who trades in Frigates of the second Rate?
And yet some Care of S—st should be had,
Nothing so mean for which he can't run mad;
His Wit confirms him but a Slave the more,
And makes a Princess whom he found a Whore.
The Youth might save much Trouble and Expence,
Were he a Dupe of only common Sense.

But here's his point; 'A Wench (he cries) for me!
I never touch a Dame of Quality.'

    To *Palmer's* Bed no Actress comes amiss,
He courts the whole *Personae Dramatis*:
He too can say, 'With Wives I never sin.'
But Singing-Girls and Mimicks draw him in.
Sure, worthy Sir, the Diff'rence is not great,
With *whom* you lose your Credit and Estate?
This, or that Person, what avails to shun?
What's wrong is wrong, wherever it be done:
The Ease, Support, and Lustre of your Life,
Destroy'd alike with Strumpet, Maid, or Wife.

    What push'd poor *Ellis* on th' Imperial Whore?
'Twas but to be where *Charles* had been before.
The fatal Steel unjustly was apply'd,
When not his Lust offended, but his Pride:
Too hard a Penance for defeated Sin,
Himself shut out, and *Jacob Hall* let in.

    Suppose that honest Part that rules us all,
Should rise, and say—'Sir *Robert*! or Sir *Paul*!
Did I demand, in my most vig'rous hour,
A Thing descended from the Conqueror?
Or when my pulse beat highest, ask for any
Such Nicety, as Lady or Lord *Fanny*?'—
What would you answer? Could you have the Face,
When the poor Suff'rer humbly mourn'd his Case,
To cry 'You weep the Favours of her *Grace*?'

    Hath not indulgent Nature spread a Feast,
And giv'n enough for Man, enough for Beast?
But Man corrupt, perverse in all his ways,
In search of Vanities from Nature strays:
Yea, tho' the Blessing's more than he can use,
Shun the permitted, the forbid pursues!

Weigh well the Cause from whence these Evils
    spring,
'Tis in thyself, and not in God's good Thing:
Then, lest Repentence punish such a Life,
Never, ah, never! kiss thy Neighbour's Wife.
    First, Silks and Diamonds veil no finer Shape,
Or plumper Thigh, than lurk in humble Crape:
And *secondly*, how innocent a *Belle*
Is she who shows what Ware she has to sell;
Not Lady-like, displays a milk-white Breast,
And hides in sacred Sluttishness the rest.
    Our ancient Kings (and sure those Kings were wise,
Who judg'd themselves, and saw with their own
    Eyes)
A War-horse never for the Service chose,
But ey'd him round, and stript off all the Cloaths;
For well they knew, proud Trappings serve to hide
A heavy Chest, thick Neck, or heaving Side.
But Fools are ready Chaps, agog to buy,
Let but a comely Fore-hand strike the Eye:
No Eagle sharper, every Charm to find,
To all defects, *Ty—y* not so blind:
Goose-rump'd, Hawk-nose'd, Swan-footed, is my
    Dear?
They'l praise her *Elbow*, *Heel*, or *Tip o' th' Ear*.
    A Lady's Face is all you see undress'd;
(For none but Lady M— shows the Rest)
But if to Charms more latent you pretend,
What Lines encompass, and what Works defend!
Dangers on Dangers! obstacles by dozens!
Spies, Guardians, Guests, old Women, Aunts, and
    Cozens!
Could you directly to her Person go,
Stays will obstruct above, and Hoops below,

And if the Dame says yes, the Dress says no.
Not thus at *N—dh—m's*; your judicious Eye
May measure there the Breast, the Hip, the Thigh!
And will you run to Perils, Sword, and Law,
All for a Thing you ne're so much as *saw*?
      'The Hare once seiz'd the Hunter heeds no more
The little Scut he so pursu'd before,
Love follows flying Game (as *Sucklyn* sings)
And 'tis for that the wonton Boy has Wings.'
Why let him Sing—but when you're in the Wrong,
Think ye to cure the Mischief with a Song?
Has Nature set no bounds to wild Desire?
No Sense to guide, no Reason to enquire,
What solid Happiness, what empty Pride?
And what is best indulg'd, or best deny'd?
If neither Gems adorn, nor Silver tip
The flowing Bowl, will you not wet your Lip?
When sharp with Hunger, scorn you to be fed,
Except on *Pea-Chicks*, at the *Bedford-head*?
Or, when a tight, neat Girl, will serve the Turn,
In errant Pride continue stiff, and burn?
I'm a plain Man, whose Maxim is profest,
'The Thing at hand is of all Things the *best*.'
But Her who will, and then will not comply,
Whose Word is *If*, *Perhaps*, and *By-and-By*,
Z—ds! let some Eunuch or Platonic take—
So *B—t* cries, Philosopher and Rake!
Who asks no more (right reasonable Peer)
Than not to wait too long, nor pay too dear.
Give me a willing Nymph! 'tis all I care,
Extremely clean, and tolerably fair,
Her Shape her own, whatever Shape she have,
And just that White and Red which Nature gave.
Her I transported touch, transported view,

And call her *Angel*! *Goddess*! *Montague*!
No furious Husband thunders at the Door;
No barking Dog, no Household in a Roar;
From gleaming Swords no shrieking Women run;
No wretched Wife cries out, *Undone*! *Undone*?
Seiz'd in the Fact, and in her Cuckold's Pow'r,
She kneels, she weeps, and worse! resigns her
      Dow'r.
Me, naked me, to Posts, to Pumps they draw,
To shame eternal, or eternal Law.
Oh Love! be deep Tranquility my Luck!
No Mistress *H—ysh—m* near, no Lady *B—ck*!
For, to be taken, is the Dev'll in Hell;
This Truth, let *L—l, J—ys, O—w* tell.

BENJAMIN FRANKLIN

Advice on the Choice of a Mistress

This classic piece of Franklin wit could not be found in any "respectable" edition of his complete works until modern times. Noel Perrin, author of *Dr. Bowdler's Legacy*, notes that Franklin is "probably the leading native victim of bowdlerism, since during the nineteenth century he was almost the only American writer who was both unprotected by copyright and the author of anything expurgable."

✳   ✳   ✳

Philadelphia, June 25, 1745

My dear Friend:

I know of no medicine fit to diminish the violent natural inclinations you mention, and if I did, I think I should not communicate it to you. Marriage is the proper remedy. It is the most natural state of man, and therefore the state in which you are most likely to find solid happiness. Your reasons against entering into it at present appear to me not well founded. The circumstantial advantages you have in view by postponing it are not only uncertain, but they are small in comparison with that of the thing itself, the being married and settled. It is the man and woman united that make the complete human being. Separate, she wonts his force of body and strength of reason; he, her softness, sensibility, and acute discernment. Together they are more likely to succeed in the world. A single man has not nearly the value he would have in the state of union. He is an incomplete animal. He resembles the odd half of a pair of scissors. If you get a prudent, healthy wife, your industry in your profession, with her good economy, will be a fortune sufficient.

But if you will *not* take this counsel and persist in thinking a commerce with the sex inevitable, then I repeat my former advice, that in all your amours you should prefer old women to young ones.

You call this a paradox and demand my reasons. They are these:

1. Because they have more knowledge of the world and their minds are better stored with observations, their conversation is more improving and more lastingly agreeable.

2. Because when women cease to be handsome they study to be good. To maintain their influence over men, they supply the diminution of beauty by an augmentation of utility. They learn to do a thousand services small and great, and are the most tender and useful of friends when you are sick. Thus they continue amiable. And

hence there is hardly such a thing to be found as an old woman who is not a good woman.

3. Because there is no hazard of children, which irregularly produced may be attended with much inconvenience.

4. Because through more experience they are more prudent and discreet in conducting an intrigue to prevent suspicion. The commerce with them is therefore safer with regard to your reputation. And with regard to theirs, if the affair should happen to be known, considerate people might be rather inclined to excuse an old woman, who would kindly take care of a young man, form his manners by her good counsels, and prevent his ruining his life and fortune among mercenary prostitutes.

5. Because in every animal that walks upright the deficiency of the fluids that fill the muscles appears first in the highest part. The face first grows lank and wrinkled; then the neck, then the breast and arms; the lower parts continuing to the last as plump as ever: so that covering all above with a basket, and regarding only what is below the girdle, it is impossible of two women to tell an old one from a young one. And as in the dark all cats are gray, the pleasure of corporal enjoyment with an old woman is at least equal, and frequently superior; every knack being, by practice, capable of improvement.

6. Because the sin is less. The debauching a virgin may be her ruin, and make her for life unhappy.

7. Because the compunction is less. The having made a young girl miserable may give you a frequent bitter reflection; none of which can attend the making an old woman happy.

8th and lastly. They are so grateful!

Thus much for my paradox. But still I advise you to marry directly; being sincerely

Your affectionate friend,

Benjamin Franklin

WALT WHITMAN

Leaves of Grass

Whitman, a towering figure in American poetry, was an iconoclast first and foremost. His earthy approach to sexual themes aroused the most fury during his lifetime, but his celebrations of nature, nonconformity, and individualism were often his critics' real targets.

The legendary 1855 collection *Leaves of Grass*, in which this excerpt appears, faced overt suppression for decades; a district attorney in Boston threatened the book's publisher with criminal prosecution if the book was not expurgated. It was instead withdrawn from the city limits. Upon the volume's initial release, only one American library dared purchase a copy; now, nearly a century and a half later, there are still libraries unwilling to include Whitman's masterpiece in their collections.

✳　✳　✳

From pent-up, aching rivers;
From that of myself, without which I were nothing;
From what I am determined to make illustrious,
      even if I stand sole among men;
From my own voice resonant — singing the phallus,
Singing the song of procreation,
Singing the need of superb children, and therein
      superb grown people,
Singing the muscular urge and the blending,
Singing the bedfellow's song, (O resistless yearning!
O for any and each, the body correlative attracting!
O for you, whoever you are, your correlative body!
      O it, more than all else, you delighting!)
— From the hungry gnaw that eats me night and
      day;
From native moments — from bashful pains —
      singing them;
Singing something yet unfound, though I have
      diligently sought it, many a long year,
Singing the true song of the Soul, fitful, at random;
Singing what, to the Soul, entirely redeemed her, the
      faithful one, even the prostitute, who detained
      me when I went to the city;
Singing the song of prostitutes;
Renascent with grossest Nature, or among animals;
Of that — of them, and what goes with them, my
      poems informing;
Of the smell of apples and lemons — of the pairing
      of birds,
Of the wet of woods — of the lapping of waves,
Of the mad pushes of waves upon the land — I
      them chanting:
The overture lightly sounding — the strain
      anticipating;

The welcome nearness — the sight of the perfect
      body;
The swimmer swimming naked in the bath, or
      motionless on his back lying and floating;
The female form approaching — I, pensive,
      love-flesh tremulous, aching;
The divine list, for myself or you, or for any one,
      making;
The face — the limbs — the index from head to
      foot, and what it arouses;
The mystic deliria — the madness amorous — the
      utter abandonment;
(Hark close, and still, what I now whisper to you,
I love you — O you entirely possess me,
O I wish that you and I escape from the rest, and go
      utterly off — O free and lawless,
Two hawks in the air — two fishes swimming in the
      sea not more lawless than we;)
— The furious storm through me careering — I
      passionately trembling;
The oath of the inseparableness of two together —
      of the woman that loves me, and whom I love
      more than my life — that oath swearing;
(O I willingly stake all, for you!
O let me be lost, if it must be so!
O you and I — what is it to us what the rest do or
      think?
What is all else to us? only that we enjoy each
      other, and exhaust each other, if it must be so:)
— From the master — the pilot I yield the vessel to;
The general commanding me, commanding all —
      from him permission taking;
From time the programme hastening, (I have
      loitered too long, as it is);

From sex — From the warp and from the woof;
(To talk to the perfect girl who understands me,
To waft to her these from my own lips — to effuse
      them from my own body;)
From privacy — from frequent repinings alone;
From plenty of persons near, and yet the right
      person not near;
From the soft sliding of hands over me, and
      thrusting of fingers through my hair and beard;
From the long sustained kiss upon the mouth or
      bosom;
From the close pressure that makes me or any man
      drunk, fainting with excess;
From what the divine husband knows — from the
      work of fatherhood;
From exultation, victory, and relief — from the
      bedfellow's embrace in the night;
From the act-poems of eyes, hands, hips, and
      bosoms,
From the cling of the trembling arm,
From the bending curve and the clinch,
From side by side, the pliant coverlid off-throwing,
From the one so unwilling to have me leave — and
      me just as unwilling to leave,
(Yet a moment, O tender waiter, and I return;)
— From the hour of shining stars and dropping
      dews,
From the night, a moment, I, emerging, flitting out,
Celebrate you, act divine — and you, children
      prepared for,
And you, stalwart loins.

LONGFELLOW
AND
THE ALGONQUIN INDIANS

Hiawatha

and

The Origin of Manabozho

The Algonquin folk myth of the origin of the trickster Man-abozho is part of the basis of Henry Wadsworth Longfel-low's famous poem *Hiawatha.* It is interesting to compare the two and see what deletions to the frank story Longfel-low felt were necessary for his audience.

❉   ❉   ❉

FROM LONGFELLOW'S *HIAWATHA*
    Fair Nokomis bore a daughter.
    And she called her name Wenonah,
    As the first-born of her daughters.
    And the daughter of Nokomis
    Grew up like the prairie lilies,

Grew a tall and slender maiden,
With the beauty of the moonlight,
With the beauty of the starlight.
        And Nokomis warned her often,
Saying oft, and oft repeating,
"Oh, beware of Mudjekeewis;
Of the west-wind Mudjekeewis,
Listen not to what he tells you;
Lie not down upon the meadow,
Stoop not down among the lilies,
Lest the West-Wind come and harm you!"
        But she heeded not the warning,
Heeded not those words of wisdom.
And the West-Wind came at evening,
Walking lightly o'er the prairie,
Whispering to the leaves and blossoms,
Bending low the flowers and grasses,
Found the beautiful Wenonah
Lying there among the lilies,
Wooed her with his words of sweetness,
Wooed her with his soft caresses,
Till she bore a son in sorrow,
Bore a son of love and sorrow.
        Thus was born my Hiawatha,
Thus was born the child of wonder . . .

* * *

FROM THE ALGONQUIN INDIANS' *THE ORIGIN OF MANABOZHO*

Long ago, all things were young, and in a certain place lived an old woman and her daughter. The girl had no husband; her mother had premonitions and was sure that some evil would come to the girl, and so was extremely careful about her. The mother had heard in a dream that the child was in grave danger if she ever once faced in the direction of the setting sun. Each time the girl went out to do so much as relieve herself, she had to mind her mother's rules on this matter—even after she grew to womanhood.

One day, however, the daughter went alone into the woods on a foggy day and got lost. As she wandered in search of the way back to her home, she felt the need to urinate. She stopped and went about the business—but, alas, faced the wrong direction. She had a strange feeling as she squatted there; simultaneously, a great whirlwind blew into her, sending her clothing over her head and leaving her naked from the waist down. The wind died away, and she covered herself hastily and found her way home. When she returned, she told her mother what had happened and of her odd feelings. The young woman's mother turned to face her daughter and declared that a great tragedy had now fallen upon the family. The young woman was terrified when her mother asked her if she had faced in the wrong direction.

"I did," the young woman replied, "but it was an accident. I know I will suffer. I can tell even as I speak to you that I am pregnant."

As time went on, it became clear that the young woman would indeed suffer. More than one baby was within her, and great struggling was evident. She was in severe pain. The babies were fighting each other for domination within her body, for posession of the power that had passed into her. One could hear the children arguing from inside her womb. A voice would call out, "I am first," and another would say the same, and another in turn. Then the children would fight terribly. When her time arrived, she underwent a greater struggle than ever, and the fighting increased to a horrific level. The young woman was torn asunder by the battling children, and pieces of her were scattered in all directions, to the end of space. The young woman's mother found herself blown many miles away. The children who emerged were the four winds—and Manabozho, now the unyielding east wind, emerged as the first of his brethren.

ALGERNON CHARLES SWINBURNE

Love and Sleep

The collection in which these poems appear was hastily
withdrawn by Swinburne's publisher when critic Robert
Buchanan denounced it as belonging to "the fleshly
school." Swinburne's open letter to Buchanan, *The
Devil's Due*, was suppressed as well, due to concerns
that it was libelous in nature.

✳ ✳ ✳

Lying asleep between the strokes of night
      I saw my love lean over my sad bed,
      Pale as the duskiest lily's leaf or head,
   Smooth-skinned and dark, with bare throat made to
      bite,
Too wan for blushing and too warm for white,
      But perfect-coloured without white or red.
      And her lips opened amorously, and said—
I wist not what, saving one word—Delight.
And all her face was honey to my mouth,
      And all her body pasture to mine eyes;

The long lithe arms and hotter hands than fire,
The quivering flanks, hair smelling of the south,
The bright light feet, the splendid supple thighs
    And glittering eyelids of my soul's desire.

PAUL VERLAINE

Partie Carrée

Verlaine's widely circulated works raised some eyebrows
in his day. This poem from his long-suppressed private
collection had, until recently, only a limited—but, presumably, enthusiastic—audience.

✳   ✳   ✳

The hollow of the back, the hollow of immature
        dreams, chaste:
Oh, ass—adored throne of lechers!
Ass, whose curves are transplendent with pure
        whiteness,
Your cheeks beam triumphant, more magnificent
        than any face!

Breasts, twin milky, azure mountains, with darkened
        summits
That look out over the valley and the sacred
        meadow!

Breasts, whose tips offer the living fruit of love,
    savored
By lips and tongues drunk with good fortune!

Ass, creviced with a rosy shadow, dark,
The spot where ardor, mad, lingers.
Cheeks, dear pillows whose ample fold welcomes
    the face,
The cock, haven of hands after their countless
    adventures!

Breasts, terminus for hands bearing delicacies,
Massive, heavy breasts, that mock me in their pride;
Poised, they sway luciously, swollen and victorious
Tits over us as we kneel together. What a sight!

Ass, whose cheeks are truly the older sisters of the
    breasts,
But more at home with me, more amiable, smiling
    as well,
Lacking any of the mischevious, the sense of wily
    domination,
Your lovelieness is its own supremacy.

Lovely dictators, the four of you together,
My queens, my monarchs, those the peasants bow
    before,
As you oil the heads of your beloved ones, your
    worshipers,
Hear our shouts of praise and devotion, divine
    breasts, royal ass!

Censorship Is Part of the Past . . . or Is It?

Following is a list of some of the more notable works that were banned or suppressed as a result of perceived indelicacy or obscenity not so very long ago.

✳   ✳   ✳

On its release in 1885, Mark Twain's *The Adventures of Huckleberry Finn* was banned by the Concord, Massachusetts public library. Library officials considered the book to represent "trash . . . suitable only for the slums"—an apparent reference to the work's mildly colorful language. The book, considered by many to be the greatest and most influential book ever written by an American, still regularly runs afoul of school librarians who refuse to stock unexpurgated editions.

✳   ✳   ✳

In 1895, The New England Watch and Ward Society banned the sale of the playscript of Oscar Wilde's drama *Salome,* as it felt the work would tend to corrupt the morals of its readers. The group later forced the cancellation of a planned Boston production of Richard Strauss's opera *Salome.*

∗   ∗   ∗

In 1921, a New York physician was arrested and convicted of selling "obscene literature"—contraceptive activist Marie Stopes' *Married Love.*

∗   ∗   ∗

John Steinbeck's *The Grapes of Wrath* was banned in St. Louis, Kansas City, and parts of Oklahoma and California in the late 1930s.

∗   ∗   ∗

Henrik Ibsen's *Ghosts*, a landmark drama that criticized conventional societal mores, was refused a license for production by English authorities in the 1890s on the grounds that it dealt with venereal disease and was therefore obscene. As late as 1939, the play was heavily expurgated by the Spanish government.

✳   ✳   ✳

Foreign-printed copies of James Joyce's masterwork *Ulysses*, perhaps the greatest work of literature of the twentieth century, were seized by United States customs officials as late as 1933. (The seizure was later ruled improper in a landmark legal case that opened the door for the book's mainstream release.)

✳   ✳   ✳

In 1944, a mail-order publisher was ordered by New York postal authorities to blot out references in its catalog to materials the authorities considered obscene (such as a paperback edition of Voltaire's *Candide*). The order was obeyed, the catalogs were altered, and the approved mail was delivered.

✳   ✳   ✳

William Faulkner's books *Mosquitoes, Sanctuary,* and *The Wild Palms* were seized from commercial bookstores by the Philadelphia Vice Squad in 1948. The raid was upheld by Pennsylvania courts even after Faulkner won the Nobel prize for literature in 1950.

✳   ✳   ✳

Massachusetts courts banned Erskine Caldwell's *God's Little Acre* from the state in 1950.

* * *

A House of Representatives Subcommittee on Appropriations denied funding for reprints of the government publication *Profile of America* because it contained, among other suspect passages, an excerpt from Eugene O'Neill's *Strange Interlude* considered by committee members to be obscene.

* * *

Theodore Dreiser's classic *Sister Carrie* was banned in the state of Vermont until 1958.

* * *

The California community of Riverside ordered all of the works of Ernest Hemingway removed from its school libraries in 1960.

* * *

In 1966, future North Carolina Senator Jesse Helms

forced the firing of a college teacher who had assigned Andrew Marvell's poem "To His Coy Mistress" to students.

✳   ✳   ✳

High school administrators in Minnesota were physically attacked in 1968 by a group protesting the school's inclusion of J.D. Salinger's *The Catcher in the Rye* in the school library.

✳   ✳   ✳

The National Coalition Against Censorship listed among many others the following books as subjects of censorship litigation in the mid-1980s:

The Bell Jar, Sylvia Plath
The Best Short Stories by Negro Writers, Langston
     Hughes, ed.
A Clockwork Orange, Anthony Burgess
The Fixer, Bernard Malamud
One Flew Over the Cuckoo's Nest, Ken Kesey
Our Bodies, Ourselves, Boston Women's Health
     Collective
Slaughterhouse-Five, Kurt Vonnegut
Young and Black in America, Alexander and Lester,
     eds.

* * *

In 1987, censorship groups used an extraordinarily broad reading of an amendment sponsored by Utah Senator Orrin Hatch to support the banning of John Steinbeck's *Of Mice and Men* from public schools in Texas and Missouri.

* * *

In the fall of 1991, the U.S. Senate overwhelmingly approved an amendment prohibiting the National Endowment for the Arts from awarding grants for any work that describes or depicts "sexual or excretory activities or organs" in a way that could be interpreted as "offensive."

* * *

Bibliography

Noble, William. *Bookbanning in America: Who Bans Books?—and Why*. Middlebury, VT: Paul S. Erickson, 1990.

Burress, Lee. *Battle of the Books: Literary Censorship in the Public Schools, 1950-1985*. Metuchen, NJ and London: The Scarecrow Press, Inc., 1989.

Hentoff, Nat. *The First Freedom: The Tumultuous History of Free Speech in America*. New York: Delacorte Press, 1980.

Coffin, Tristram Potter. *The Proper Book of Sexual Folklore*. New York: Continuum, 1977.

Haight, Anne Lyon. *Banned Books: Informal Notes on Some Books Banned for Various Reasons at Various Times and Various Places*. New York and London: R.R. Bowker Company, 1970.

Perrin, Noel. *Dr. Bowdler's Legacy: A History of Expurgated Books in England and America*. New York: Atheneum, 1969.

Rembar, Charles. *The End of Obscenity*. New York: Random House, 1968.

Loth, David. *The Erotic in Literature: A Historical Survey of Pornography as Delightful as It Is Indiscreet*. London: Secker and Warburg, 1961.

Untermeyer, Louis (ed.). *A Treasury of Ribaldry*. Garden City, NY: Hanover House, 1956.

Index